DE LUCA

THE SINISTER GAME

The Men of Mayhem
Book Three

CHELLE ROSE

To those of you who seek to numb the pain.
Somedays it hurts too much. The never-ending feeling of being inadequate.
Please believe me…
You are fucking enough. Those that said you weren't, lied. Now be a good girl and stop lying to yourself.

"I'm selfish, impatient and a little insecure. I make mistakes, I am out of control and at times hard to handle. But if you can't handle me at my worst, then you sure as hell don't deserve me at my best."
-Marilyn Monroe

TRIGGER WARNINGS:

Drug Trafficking
Drug Use
Addiction
Bullying (Not MMC's)
Coercion
Bondage
Blackmail
Graphic Sexual Content
Violence
Murder
Kidnapping
Two MMCs (brothers) Share the FMC
Criminal Activity
Bribery
Facial (Not the spa kind)
Abuse (Not the MMC)
Abduction of an Infant
Possible Eating Disorder

If you are a victim of sexual assault, you do not have to suffer alone.

National Sexual Assault Hotline – 800.656.HOPE (4673)
The hotline provides emotional support, advice and crisis intervention and through local partnerships callers can receive immediate help in their community.
National Sexual Assault Online Hotline – online.rainn.org
The online hotline provides support, advice, and crisis intervention through a secure instant-messaging format. For help in Spanish, visit rainn.org/es.

National Domestic Violence Hotline – 1.800.787.7233 or www.thehotline.org

The hotline provides 24/7 confidential, one-on-one support to each caller, offering crisis assistance and information about next steps. Bilingual advocates are on hand, and the Language Line offers translations in 170+ different languages.

Americans Overseas Domestic Violence Crisis Center And the Sexual Assault Support & Help For Americans Abroad Program – 866.USWOMEN (879.6636)
The crisis center can be reached internationally toll-free from 175 countries, serving both civilian and military populations overseas. Advocates can be reached 24/7 by first dialing your AT&T USADirect access number and at the prompt, enter the phone number: 866-USWOMEN (879-6636).

Chapter One

NATALIA

Twelve first dates and zero second ones can leave a girl feeling more inadequate than usual. I've never felt like I'm enough, so it's not entirely new. It stings. What am I doing that makes none of these men want to see me again? There must be something I'm doing or not doing, but I've gone through it a thousand times in my mind, and every time, I come up empty-handed. I don't know why I am constantly ghosted.

The excitement you usually feel when getting ready for a first date isn't present on date number thirteen. Three months. Thirteen dates. I should probably just throw in the towel, buy ten cats, and get it over with. I sit at a fancy Italian restaurant, waiting for my date, Anthony, to show up. He's ten minutes late. I don't get second dates, but being stood up is new. I glance at the ceiling and appreciate the handcrafted wine glass chandelier. The tables all have a white tablecloth and floating candles in a holder that looks like a small fishbowl. Most restaurants I've been to have a selection of booths and tables;

however, there are no booths here. Black chairs sit at each table, contrasting to the color of the tablecloths.

The server returns to me for the twentieth time. "Still waiting?"

I sigh, trying to convey how annoyed I am that she keeps asking, "I'll take another glass of wine and the bill."

The annoyance she feels is visible to her arched brow. "Yes, ma'am," she bites. As pissed as I'm sure she is that her tip will be much lower for two drinks versus two meals, I can guarantee you, it's me that's the most irritated.

My best friend is happily married, disgustingly so. I'm happy for her, and I am, but it stings watching them together and wondering if I'll never have what she does. I don't want everything she has; she's married to a mafia man. No, thank you. He has three brothers. Dante has asked me out more times than I can count. My answer has always been no. Then there's Drake, who looks at me like he wants nothing more than to kill me. Are there no good guys left?

I hand the server my credit card as she sets my wine before me. She's a pretty blonde, wearing a black skirt and a white button-down blouse. I know she'll make plenty of tips tonight based on that alone. Aren't things always easier for pretty people? I felt uncomfortable when she approached my table because she reminded me so much of Nicole. The server walks away, her heels clicking on the black marble floor as I stare at my wine and get lost in the past.

Since I was four years old, I have known I would be a dancer. A ballerina, more specifically. My life is like a tragic Cinderella story, except my sister is my twin, not my step-sister. My mother is also my biological mother, although sometimes I'm not sure if she realizes it. And there's no prince charming coming to save me from this nightmare. I'm not sad or hopeless, though. I have this. Ballet. Something happens to me when I lace up my pointe shoes. A transformation of sorts. All the insecurity and awkwardness fade away, and I become the young woman I desperately want to be. Beautiful. Elegant. Graceful. I own the stage. Ballet owns me. When I dance, it's as if all the broken shards of my soul magically slide back into place. The voices quiet while the music commands my body to move in sync with every note.

Three months ago, I was allowed to audition for Reflections, a world-renowned ballet company. In four months, they will begin their national tour of Romeo and Juliet. At fifteen, I'm younger than most of the far more experienced women here, so I don't expect to be cast as Juliet. I'm told they attempted to find a ballerina in their company but did not find the right fit. My dance teacher referred to a small selection of her students, and I'm guessing that, by the large number of bodies I see as I glance around the room, others did the same thing. When my gaze lands on my blue-eyed, perfect sister, I'm annoyed but not surprised. I'm not sure she even wants this, but she will never pass up an opportunity to take something from me. Every boy I've ever liked she has taken from me. Friends. Same thing. There has been nothing I've ever loved more than this.

I've heard it throughout the years. Sibling rivalry is what they call it, but I disagree. It's more like sibling brutality. She's cruel. Nowhere is too far for Nicole to go, as long as it hurts me.

I attempt to get Nicole out of my head because all that matters is the dance. The audition that could change the course of my life. First, we will dance our solo choreography and pair up with a male dancer for the rest of our audition. My name is called, so I look at my sister. I spot her forming the letters p-i-g on her chest, and unfortunately, I know what she's trying to remind me of. However, I keep my posture straight, hold my head high, and stand in the fourth position, waiting for the violin that I now know by heart.

I don't have to think about the next move as I spin and leap across the stage. It's all in my muscle memory. After rehearsing this piece for months, my body knows what to do next. If I haven't been dancing to it, I'm going through it in my mind, and when I'm sleeping, I dream about it. The most challenging part of this choreography is the twenty-two fouettes. You must pass your working leg in front or behind your body while spinning. If I don't spot correctly, I could end up dizzy and flat on my ass. I'm pleased when I execute them with perfection. Once I finish, I wait for the second part, dancing with a male dancer. That makes me nervous because if the other person messes up, so do you. It's a lot of trust to put into a perfect stranger. I breathe a sigh of relief when we finish with no issues.

Angelica Rothschild, the producer of this show, begins walking around and tapping some people on the shoulder. Are these the people that might get it? My heart races as my chest squeezes.

"If I tapped you on your shoulder, your audition is over. Thank you for your time."

I gaze at the perfection of this woman as my breathing returns to normal. She's gorgeous, poised, confident, and slender. Wearing a leotard and ballet skirt, her dark hair in a tight bun, Ms. Rothschild looks like the graceful dancer she was when she graced the stage as a prima ballerina. She retired a year ago at forty, which is old for a dancer. Most ballerinas are forced to retire between thirty-five and forty if an injury doesn't sideline them before then. Injuries are common. Ballet is strenuous and puts a great deal of stress on the body. During the thirteen years I've studied ballet, I've had minor injuries along the way, all annoying but only mildly painful.

Twelve of us left after she dismissed most of the room. My heart thumps like it's preparing to leap out of my chest.

I learned I got the lead a few days later, but there was bad news. Nicole is my alternate. If I'm injured, she will take my spot. Without a doubt, I know she's praying for an injury. We both practice in the same rehearsal studio, although in different rooms. The room is lined with mirrors, and a bar runs along the wall. I stand with one leg on the bar as I stretch when I hear footsteps approach.

"Hey pig," she says without venom, like it's just an obvious statement. It's not new to hear that word from her; she decided that was my nickname when we were eight, and I developed breasts earlier than expected, earlier than her. Maybe it came from jealousy, or perhaps she truly sees me that way; in either case, it doesn't change how it makes me feel. When we were younger, I used to tell myself that pig stood for a pretty intelligent girl. As time passed, I believed my little mantra less and less. The pretty girl I once saw in the mirror faded. Every flaw became apparent as my internal voice became Nicole, reminding me I'd never be good enough and that I was, in fact, a pig. A fat, disgusting pig.

She grins when I don't respond to her like she won some sort of contest. Running her hand along the bar, she smiles sweetly, "Careful. It would be terrible if you got injured. Heartbreaking."

Then she turned and walked out of the room. While she didn't threaten me, somehow, I knew something was coming. With Nicole, there always is. It's a rare day that passes without some form of bullying from her. When did it start? Early.

From the moment I was born, my twin sister hated me. It's sad, but it's true. I still don't know why, but I don't understand why my parents seem to feel the same way. Nicole does everything right, while I do everything wrong. We are fraternal twins, so we aren't supposed to look like carbon copies of each other, but we don't even look like sisters. She's tall, thin, and blonde. She's stunning and always gets the attention of any man in the room. It's always been that way. I have dark hair, am short, and, according to my sister, I'm fat and should be disgusted with myself. The only thing we ever had in common was ballet.

We got matching pink leotards, skirts, ballet shoes, and dance lessons on our fourth birthday.

Miss Leah calls out, "Third position, Demi Plie."

We switch from first to third, some more effortlessly than others. She walks over to Nicole and says, "Heels on the floor. Knees over your feet."

My sister glared at me as if I was the reason she was messing up. To make matters worse, Miss Leah says, "Watch Natalia and then try again."

After we got home from dance class, Mom was angry with me. My sister got ice cream while I was sent to my room, which was my punishment for showing off.

My mother and sister are two peas in a pod, identical. It's always them against me, like the home version of mean girls in high school. My dad just goes with whatever my mom says. He never makes eye contact with me, as if he hates me as much as they do. I live my life as an outsider while feigning smiles and confidence. Only one person knows even a sliver of my pain. Giada. When we moved here from Florida, she quickly became my saving grace. She sees me. She sees Nicole for who she is—my tormentor. I'm grateful to have her. I crave the one thing I've never had. Love from my family. My sister. Twins are supposed to have some magical link to each other, feel each other's pain, and have an unbreakable bond.

Chapter Two

DANTE

May 23, 2014

Today is the worst day of my life. I wish I were dead.

Natalia's bookshelf is lined with journals, each with a year stitched onto the outside. I started with the first one, labeled 2014 because I figured I should start at the beginning to learn everything about her.

That was a brief entry etched with heartbreak. Not only that, but it also has a dried bloody handprint on it. I want to turn the page and find out what she wrote next, but the pages are glued together with blood. If I rip it, she'll know someone was here. It's too early to show our hand, so that can't happen yet.

"Well, that's a little dark for little Miss Sunshine," Drake says as he looks over my shoulder at the words I can't stop staring at. He runs his fingers down the bloody handprint. "What happened?"

I shrug as I snap the journal closed. "I don't know. The next several pages are stuck together, but it must've been something terrible if she hurt herself."

Placing the journal back where I found it, I turn to Drake. "Get the cameras set up?"

He nods as he walks over to the door. "We should go before she gets back."

I sigh as I look back into her home; a feeling I'm not used to washes over me, and Drake says, "She's fine. That was ten years ago."

My brother is probably right, but I want to know everything about her. What makes her happy, and what the fuck made her break to the point of attempting to take her life? Three days ago, I put Benji on finding everything he could on Natalia. We're meeting him at our warehouse shortly. The De Luca brothers own several businesses. Domenic has a nightclub, and Devil and Damian own restaurants. Drake and I have hotels. The Diamond, where we're meeting Benji tonight, has a warehouse behind the hotel. It's where we do our dirty work. None of our employees go near it; they know better. While it's never been discussed, our people know about George and the fact that he disappeared three years ago after he got a little too curious. If someone is a threat, they are eliminated. It's not that I enjoy killing people, but I don't dislike it either. Like taking the trash out; it's not a big deal. You do it because it's necessary.

Natalia would probably say I didn't need to kill all the men she's gone out with within the last couple of months, but she'd be wrong. Not every man died. It was their choice. If we say to stay away from our girl, the decision should be a simple agreement. The ones that refused paid the price for that. We haven't worked out the details because our family is complicated, but she'll be with us. Drake and I want to take her, but Domenic and Damian would lose their minds and intervene. My sister-in-law is best friends with Natalia, and if she were missing for forty-eight hours, Giada would run to my brother. For years, my brother hated me for a situation I had gotten myself into by unknowingly falling for the enemy. Jewel Aiello was the biggest mistake of my life. I was an absolute fool. We'll kill the entire Aiello family one day, but we can't move until Domenic gives the go-ahead. I don't like it, but it's how it works for the De Luca family. Domenic is the head of our family, and going against him would put us all at risk.

We walk to our cars and drive separately to the warehouse, where we meet Benji, our intel guy. He does a little of everything: hacking, surveillance, whatever we need. He knows not to mention our little pet project to Domenic or Damian. I don't trust many people outside of my brothers, but I trust him implicitly. He has been with us for years. Domenic has hacking skills, but has nothing to the level of Benji. When he needed a deeper dive into enemies than he could achieve, he found Benjamin Thorne, also known as Benji. He has never let us down, so I hope to get a clearer picture of Natalia Grant.

I speed down the street, Drake beside me in the other lane. Luckily, it's late enough that the roads aren't packed with cars. I'd rather be on my motorcycle tonight since the weather is nice for January, but I'm driving my Range Rover. Pulling in behind the hotel, I get an alert on my phone: a text message from Natalia's friend Talia.

> My date was a no-show. Do you want to blow off some steam?

> You know it, babe.

> Devil?

> I'll be here in an hour.

I smile because we all own part of the club, even though it's primarily Domenic. My brother is home with his pregnant wife, and Damian is on a romantic getaway for the weekend with his wife, Kat. After I park, I get out and walk with Drake into the warehouse to meet Benji.

This is where we keep people if we need to. It's a dark, damp warehouse except for our office, where we walk now to discuss his findings. Drake opens the door, and we step inside. My brother takes a seat behind the desk while I take a seat behind mine. Benji sits in a black leather chair between our two dark wood desks.

Benji crosses his legs and opens a folder. "She hasn't had a peaceful life, and it's a little confusing. I don't have all the pieces of this bizarre puzzle, but I'll give you what I have."

I nod, urging him to continue, and he does: "Natalia Grant has a twin sister, Nicole. Her father works in finance, and her mother is a stay-at-home mother, one of those annoying dance moms."

He sends pictures to my brother and me, so I look. Natalia and her sister look nothing alike, which is strange for twins. Nicole looks like her mother, a dead ringer, but Natalia does not. She doesn't look like her father either. Why is there no familial resemblance?

"They both began dance classes at Ridgeway Ballet Academy at four."

Is our girl a dancer? I know she plays the piano, but this is news to me. I don't like not knowing this basic information about her. Glancing at Drake, he appears to think the same thing as he rubs his thumb over his beard.

"I didn't know she danced."

Benji shakes his head, "She doesn't. Not anymore. She was outstanding until someone took a bat to her knees."

Instantly, I see red. Who the fuck would do that to her? Drake mirrors my rage and barks, "Who?"

With a shrug, Benji says, "I don't know. The police took her statement, but all she knew was it was a man in dark clothing wearing a ski mask. After the attack, she was placed on a psychiatric hold, the first of many."

I clench my jaw but grit out, "Why?"

His eyes dart between mine and Drake's before he answers, "I don't know, but I feel like there's something involved with this family. Something isn't right. I hacked into the psychiatric records, and I don't know if she still does, but she was a cutter."

Glancing over at Drake, I see he's thinking the same thing I am. Dalia was a cutter for a while after our mom died. Dalia was a little kid and watched our mom get raped and beaten repeatedly until she passed away in captivity. My sister was also raped brutally. When we rescued her, she began dealing with the emotional pain by cutting her skin. We never understood it. Our way of handling pain is frequently to inflict hurt, but not to ourselves. She once explained to me that the physical pain for a few moments makes the emotional hurt subside. 'When I cut, I don't hear her crying,' she told me.

"I'm sending you a picture of Natalia's senior prom."

I glance down at my phone when the image appears. Natalia stands in a light blue dress, tears running down her face and the word pig in what seems to be spray paint on her chest. Three other girls hold her hands behind her back.

Benji says, "The blonde on the left is her sister, Nicole."

This is fucking confusing. I don't understand it. My family has always been close. Even when Domenic was pissed at me, he wouldn't have ever hurt me. I still would've had his protection had I needed it.

Chapter Three

NATALIA

Dating sucks. Anthony never showed, but I'll be damned if I let my black dress go to waste. In preparation, I got ready, did my hair and makeup, and even shaved, just in case. I have not had sex in six months and three days. I will not turn it down if a one-night stand presents itself tonight. Well, as long as it's not a troll offering. I'm not that desperate.

I miss going out with Giada, but a club isn't enjoyable when pregnant. Besides, I doubt Papa Bear would allow it. Most women would say Domenic De Luca is a red flag, and I suppose he is a little crazy about his wife. He's not trying to control her, he just wants her to be safe. After she was kidnapped for a year, I got it. That year was terrible. None of us wants to go through that again. If he can prevent it, nothing like that will ever happen again.

After pulling up to the Valet, I park, grab my purse, and step out of the vehicle, "Be good to Norma Jean," I say to the attendant, who stares at me in confusion.

"My car is Norma Jean."

Did I name my Mazda Miata after Marilyn Monroe? Of course, I did. How could I not? She was quoted as saying she was insecure her entire life. I can't imagine a woman like her having a single insecurity, but she did. I think that part of her has always called to me. It made her seem incredibly human.

I hand him my keys, and he chuckles uncomfortably. "I promise to be careful with her, ma'am."

"Gross. Don't call women ma'am. It makes us feel old."

I giggle when the young man blushes, too cute, and runs off when I spot Talia standing at the entrance waiting for me. After the door attendant scans our ID, we grab a table before they're all taken. The server brings our first and second round of drinks—a shot of tequila for both of us and a margarita.

"What are the rules tonight, Nat?"

I laugh because I always have rules about if I get drunk. Don't let me do something I'll regret because I haven't wanted just to have sex. I've aimed far too high, thinking my soulmate is looking for me somewhere. He's not. Reality has sunk in.

"No rules. I'm getting laid tonight."

She holds up her shot glass, and I do the same. We clink our glasses together as Talia says, "Cheers to finding someone to make the kitty purr."

After we down our shots, Talia declares we need to dance. My surgeon was right; I could never dance again professionally. This is as close as it gets. I rise from my chair, join Talia on the dance floor, and let the music seep into my soul as I've done a million times before. I sway my hips to the music as my friend does the same. The song started with a drum beat I've never heard, but I know it well as it continues. *I Knew You Were Trouble* by *Taylor Swift*. We continue to dance and sing along loudly when Talia moves closer to me and shouts in my ear, "A hot man is staring at you!"

I turn around slowly to a penetrating gaze I know well.

Dante De Luca. Dangerous, delicious, and hot as sin. Talia whispers in my ear, "Jesus, Nat. He's hot. If you don't fuck him, I will."

He holds his hand up and motions for me to walk over to him, so I do. I'd like to blame it on the alcohol, but after one shot and half a margarita, I really can't. My heart pounds as I approach him. I'm trapped in his stare, like some physical force pulls me to him. Leaning down, he speaks directly into my ear, which quickly travels to my core. "That's my girl."

He takes my hand and pulls me out of the club area down a hallway; I glance around and realize we're outside the bathrooms.

Pushing me up against the wall, his eyes drop to my lips. "Are you ready?"

"For what?"

Dante grabs my arms and pins my hands against the wall above my head. "Let me make you feel good."

I open my mouth to say no, but I don't fight him when he presses his lips to mine. Instead, I slide my tongue against his as he swallows my moans.

DANTE

Tasting her hasn't squashed my obsession with her. If anything, it makes me more hungry for everything her body offers. Dropping one of my hands, I slide my fingers down her side until I reach her mostly bare thigh. I'm glad she chose this tiny dress tonight, but I don't like that other men have seen her like this. I kick her feet further apart and reach under her black dress, press my fingers over her panties, pinch her clit, and she moans into my mouth. Pulling back from our kiss, I stare at her expression, wide eyes staring at me with confusion as I circle her clit with my thumb. I can read her like a dirty little book. She wants to run but can't because she likes my touch. Natalia wants more.

"I can make you come so hard, but not here. Come with me."

She gasps for breath like I've been cutting off her air. I have not.

"Just once, Dante. I told you I'm not dating you."

I nod in agreement because I know something she doesn't. Tonight, she'll be ruined. If she found it hard to find men before, this will only worsen it. Even if I let any man who wants to touch her in the future live, they'd never measure up. I keep that information to myself because I'm not prepared to kidnap her yet.

"Go tell your friend you're leaving."

I watch her closely while she goes to Talia and hugs her. I don't miss how her friend's gaze sweeps down the length of my body. She's pretty, but she's not Natalia. I approach her and take her hand. "Let's go."

"My car," she exclaims out in a near panic.

"I'll take care of it. Every need you have will be handled when you're with me."

I escort her to my waiting vehicle; I open the back door and let her slide in before I join her and instruct my driver to go to the house.

She pulls her bottom lip between her teeth and fidgets with her fingers on her lap. Natalia is a bundle of anxiety. This isn't news to me. I watch her enough to know she's riddled with insecurity. She hides it quickly with a perfect smile for most people, but I don't miss much. I didn't need Benji to tell me she was a little lost and damaged. Like the predator I am, I saw the desperation in her a mile away. The one thing Natalia wants more than anything is to be accepted for the person she is, flaws and all. Isn't that the case for all of us? She can't see beyond the mafia connection. We are dangerous men, so she's vowed to steer clear of my brother and me. If this little plan that Drake concocted doesn't work, we must forcefully make it happen.

I lean and scrape my teeth down her neck, "Relax, Sunshine. I'm going to take care of you. There's nothing to be afraid of."

She instantly relaxes with a moan when I trail my tongue down her skin. I will not fuck her here in the backseat with my driver right in front of us, but I do plan to keep her warmed up to prevent her from unraveling and begging to go home, which I have no plans of allowing.

As predicted, she has second thoughts, "This is a bad idea. I'm sorry. I can't."

I take her face, "You can and you will, Sunshine. You're going to be my good girl for tonight, and come on my fingers, my tongue and my cock."

My cock is already stiff, but when she whimpers, I nearly lose control of myself. This is what I want. What I fucking need. *Her.* Every touch. Every sound. Every orgasm. Sliding my hands into her dark hair, I tilt her head back and gaze into her brown eyes. That's what first drew me to her. If you're paying attention, you can spot every emotion running through Natalia with a glance into her eyes. I get the feeling that most people ignore her. For the life of me, I can't understand why.

Chapter Four

NATALIA

I knew this was a terrible idea the second I got into the car with Dante. There's a reason I've turned him down so many times. Now, there's no turning back as I sit in his lap, trapped in his web. His arms are wrapped around my waist, my body pulled tightly against his; I lay my head on his shoulder while his scent envelops me. I inhale the smell of spicy oranges and try to memorize it. It's intoxicating.

"You're so beautiful," he murmurs into my hair.

His words twist something in my chest as I wonder if he'd say that if he saw my sister. Every man I've ever dated ends up in bed with her and choosing her. I don't think I'm ugly, but I've never been pretty enough to hold on to someone. Nicole stole my first boyfriend when I was fourteen. Perhaps she was behind on all these first dates that never turned into second ones.

"Stop," he commands.

I lift my head and arch a questioning brow. "What?"

He smirks, "You're overthinking things. Stop."

I sigh and tell him, "This is how I am, Dante. I overthink. My anxiety controls me."

Swiping his tongue across my closed lips, he groans, "I'll be the one controlling you, Sunshine. When we tell you to come, you will. When we tell you not to, you won't."

We?

I open my mouth to ask what he means by, we but before I get a chance, the car is stopped, and his driver opens our door. Shuffling off Dantes's lap, I climb out of the vehicle with Dante beside me; he grips my hand like he's afraid I'll run away, and I probably should. While I know he kills people, I'm not worried about that. This can only be sex. I can't give him more than that because people will get hurt—namely me. I should set boundaries so I'm clear on my comfort level.

As we walk to the doorstep of his massive property, I say, "This is just sex, Dante, and only for tonight."

He spins me so I'm facing him and growls a deep throaty sound, "I told you to get out of your fucking head. Stay in the moment. Don't worry about tomorrow or the next day. Stay in the now."

Lifting my gaze to his, I breathe a breathy sigh as he runs his thumb down my cheek. Every time he touches me, a spark travels down my spine. Dante lowers his head and runs his nose along the side of my neck until his lips rest against my ear, and he speaks low, "I can't wait to devour your cunt. I won't stop until you're dripping all over my face."

I moan, and he chuckles while he takes my hand and pulls me into the house. I get a quick glimpse of the boldly decorated entryway before he quickly ushers me upstairs. When we make it into the bedroom, my heart stops as I notice the restraints on the bed. Suddenly, I realized seeing Dante in the club may not have been coincidental. Did he plan this? No, of course not. He's a bad guy, but he isn't a stalker.

"Natalia," he says in a husky voice, as if demanding my attention. My eyes dart from the king-sized bed with a dark purple comforter to his as I swallow hard. I've had sex many times with more than one man, but this feels different. Like when I walk out of here, I'll never be the same. He grabs the back of his shirt by the neck, lifts it over his head, and tosses it to the floor. Why is that so hot? My gaze travels down his muscular chest to the bulge in his pants.

"Sweet baby Jesus," I gasp, sounding like a bitch in heat. I need to calm my hormones because the wetness pooling in my now-drenched panties is ridiculous. After all, he isn't even touching me. This is all simply from looking at him.

Dante De Luca is scorching hot. His hair is longer than any of his brothers', reaching to his shoulders, and instead of being dark, it's more of a dirty blonde color. His eyes are a dark gray color that stares at me now with lust—my own drop to the tattoo that covers the left side of his neck. A rose stretched across his skin with three drops of blood on the thorns. Just above his pecs, a bigger tattoo stretches across his flesh with three roses and a skull that says De Luca in cursive.

I'm too lost in drooling over his chest to pay attention to what he's about to do. Within a fraction of a second, he grabs my shirt and rips it open, sending buttons flying everywhere.

"What the?"

He smirks at me with lust written all over his features, "Fucking beautiful," he says as he slides my shirt down my arms while staring at my lacy purple bra.

Unclasping the brass clasp on my bra, he opens it and groans, "Jesus. I knew you'd look like this. Are you ready to be my good girl?"

Because I think I'd give anything at this moment, I nod breathlessly. I want this while I swore to stay away from any De Luca brother. *I want him.*

"My brother is going to watch you come."

My eyes widen, and my heart pounds as every warning bell chimes loudly in my brain. Two of his brothers are married, so that only leaves one possibility. Drake De Luca. The biggest psychopath I've ever met. While Dante is a dangerous man, I'm not afraid of him. I believe he'd never hurt me, but Drake… He'd hurt me. I'm sure of it.

Drake comes into the room, and I'm sure this was planned. He's wearing nothing but black boxers, and suddenly, my throat swells with fear. They both have the same close-cut short beard, but Drake's hair is cut into a short crew cut. His left ear is pierced, his eyes the same gray as his brothers', and his entire upper body is covered in tattoos. All black. I stare at the barbed wire ink at the top of his chest. My gaze travels to the two tigers on his chest, down to the skulls lining his arms.

Like always, he glares at me like I've done something terrible to offend him. As if my mere existence repulses him. I have no idea what I've done to Drake to warrant this.

"Are you going to run away, pretty girl?"

I probably should do that, but I take it as a challenge instead. One I have no intention of backing down from.

"No."

I stand straighter, attempting to appear far more confident than I am, and stare back at Drake as he gazes at my bare breasts, "Why do you hate me so much? What did I do to you?"

In a split second, he grabs my throat with one hand and pushes me back until I hit the wall and grits, "You piss me off. I shouldn't want you. You're a goddamn doormat for the people you call family. You let them hurt you. I'll break you far worse than they ever could."

He grips my jaw tight and kisses me in front of his brother. The last thing I want is to be in the middle of two brothers, yet I part my lips and take his tongue into my mouth. Dante steps closer to us and brushes his thumb over my nipple, causing me to moan as Drake devours my mouth like he's wanted this for so long, but I know that can't be. His tongue moves against mine, licking every inch of my mouth in an erotic dance that leaves me breathless. I never imagined kissing Drake because he always stares at me like he's counting the ways to dismember my body. Moving to the side, he drags his tongue down my neck while Dante drops to his knees and yanks my skirt down to the floor.

"Wait. What's happening?"

Drake chuckles against my skin before biting my neck and causing me to yelp, "My brother and I are going to fucking destroy you. You'll come on our tongues, fingers, cocks, and when you cry that you can't come again, you will."

Dante rips my panties off my body, and I scold him, "Could you stop ruining my clothes?"

He laughs lightly before swiping his tongue up my slit. Sweet baby, Jesus, what's happening to me? I lost my v card a long time ago, but two men? Brothers? This is weird, and I should not be turned on like I am.

Dante slides two fingers inside me as Drake swirls his tongue over my sensitive nipples. He moves from one, then back to the other, causing me to moan repeatedly.

"Is she wet?" He asks his brother.

Dante groans, "Fucking drenched. Taste her."

They switch places, and then Drake is on his knees, plundering his tongue inside me as Dante kisses me, making me taste myself on his tongue. His hands dig into my hair as his brother fucks me with his tongue. Placing my hands on Dante's face, I moan from the feel of his beard under my fingertips. Drake sucks my clit between his lips, and I come fast and hard, banging my head against the wall.

Dante growls, "Get on the bed."

Chapter Five

DRAKE

While I remove my boxers, my brother removes his jeans and white underwear and climbs between her legs for another taste. I don't blame him one bit because she tastes sweet like honey. Right now, I want to feel her lips wrapped around my cock. I stroke myself as I walk over to her. Grabbing her shoulders, I pull her back slightly so her head hangs off the edge of the mattress. Her eyes widen with fear as a gasp escapes from her. And I fucking love it. Dante loves her already. I don't want her heart. I want to see the panic in her eyes, the struggle, and even her breath. I can't wait to see her fight. Natalia doesn't fight for a damn thing. She takes whatever abuse she's given. I want to be the man that makes her strike back. I won't be pissed when she claws at me and bites me. She'll be rewarded. I'm an asshole, so she'll never know that's the goal.

"Open wide, Pretty Girl."

She opens her mouth to question me, and I lean over her and push in between her lips. Natalia gags as I force my way to the back of her throat. Dante pins her legs and slams into her pussy. We have had an agreement for months that he fucks her pussy first. As long as I get it, there is no difference to me. Her tongue glides along my cock with every thrust, and I groan loudly when she sucks hard. I hold myself up with one hand on the mattress while I pinch her nipple, causing her to whimper on my dick. My balls hit her in the nose repeatedly, probably making it hard to breathe. And then it happens. She claws at my chest while she tries to get away. I pull back and slam into her throat over and over. After Dante comes inside her, I order him away from her pussy.

I climb onto the bed and kneel. "Over here."

She gets up and moves to me; I turn her around and pull her down onto my cock. Dante watches as she rides my dick, facing him. I know he's getting an eyeful of her bouncing tits while I rail her. Holding onto her hips, I move her up and down my length while she moans like a goddamn porn star. Her cunt squeezes my cock as she throws her head back on my shoulder and cries out in pleasure. I bury my face in her neck and inhale her sweet floral scent. Wrapping my arm around her waist, I push her forward until she's on her hands and knees. Dante doesn't waste any time; he kneels on the other end of the bed before her. He gently caresses her face while I spread her cheeks and spit onto her asshole, and push a finger into her tight hole. When she yelps in pain, Dante pushes into her mouth.

I pull back and slam back into her, my cock and finger working her at the same time. "You like this, don't you, dirty slut? You're so fucking wet."

Of course, she can't answer with Dante in her throat, but she moans around his dick, causing him to groan. I grab her hip with my free hand and fuck her hard while she whimpers, "I know you're tired, but we're not. We're going to use every fucking hole you've got until we are done."

DANTE

Her tongue glides along my cock and feels fucking unbelievable. I've fantasized about her lips wrapped around my dick countless times, but this is better than I could've ever imagined. Every moan and whimper around my length as my brother pounds into her takes me closer to the finish line. Tears run down her cheeks while I hold her head on either side and fuck her. When I hit the back of her throat, it causes tingles to rush down my spine. And then she comes. Natalia is practically screaming around my cock, and I can't hold back another second. My entire body tightens with my release, and I shoot cum down her throat. I pull out of her mouth, and she runs her tongue over my slit, licking up the leftover drops she missed. "Fucking filthy girl."

Drake pulls out of her, flips her over, pins her thighs back as he kneels behind her, and slams back into her. I sit on the bed beside her head and kiss her while running my thumb over her nipples. My tongue swipes against hers, and she runs her fingers through my hair while she moans into my mouth. Within minutes, I'm hard all over again. Natalia is like my personal Viagra. I'll never get enough. I'll never be satisfied. My dick practically screams for more.

NATALIA

I should not enjoy this as much as I am. This is weird, right? Two brothers. I've never been with one man with this much stamina, let alone two. When Drake finishes inside me, then Dante takes over, sliding back inside me with a groan.

Drake leans over, standing beside the bed, and bites my nipple, making me whimper. The pain radiates through me as it turns to pleasure. He takes my bud into his mouth and sucks hard while Dante wraps his arms around my thighs and pushes into me repeatedly.

"Fuck. This pussy is heaven," Dante groans as his cock pulses inside me.

He pulls out of me, and when I realize they're done, I say, "I'm going to take a shower and then go."

Drake chuckles. "You're not going anywhere until tomorrow. Let's get you some food, but no shower."

"No shower?"

His lips turn into a smirk as he glares at me. "No shower. You'll drip of us for fucking days."

After a trip to the bathroom, I grab a bathrobe hanging on the hook on the back of the door and put it on so I don't have to go down to the kitchen naked like the day I was born. I have had little chance to look around their house, but as I would've assumed, it speaks of the money they have. I run my fingers across the dark marble in front of the dual bathroom sinks. The walls are painted a deep red color. Whereas Domenic and Giada's house is a lot of gray, this house is far more bold in decorating. The large shower with a showerhead on two sides of the wall calls to me, but as tempting as it is, I don't get in because pissing off these two men doesn't seem like a great idea. I'll shower when I get home. I'm on birth control, so getting pregnant isn't a big concern for me. Of course, it's always possible, but it's unlikely. I should probably be concerned about diseases, but I'm not. Naïve. Stupid. Maybe. I trust them in a way that's likely dangerous for me. I giggle as I glance at the toilet with a bidet sitting beside it. Who has a bidet anyway? Someone with more money than they know what to do with.

Walking out of the bathroom and then the bedroom, I make my way to the stairs, noticing the family photographs on the wall. There are several pictures of the De Luca brothers of various ages. The most captivating one is one of a young boy smiling from ear to ear. *Drake* is imprinted in gold across it. He looks happy and friendly, completely at odds with the man I know now. I stand staring at it, wondering what changed him because now I can't imagine him truly laughing. An amused chuckle here and there, but not from happiness.

"What are you looking at, Pretty Girl?"

Hearing Drake's booming voice, I jump and quickly look at him standing in front of me with a raised eyebrow. "I was looking at the pictures and wondering what happened to you. I mean, you looked happy."

"I was happy, but nothing lasts forever."

"What happened?" I ask as I walk down the hall with him to the kitchen. He grabs my hand aggressively. "Curious, pretty girl. I'll tell you a truth for a truth of yours, but you go first."

When we enter the dining room, we join Dante at the glass table and sit in the black leather chairs. I'm not sure who made the food, but it must've already been prepared because lasagna takes a while to bake. They sit across from me as they pile lasagna, garlic bread, and a little salad onto their plates. I watch them cautiously as I put the green salad on my plate. I take a bite and thank them for the food between bites, but something makes Drake angry.

"What the fuck are you doing?"

I glance at him questioningly, because I have no idea what his problem is. He should be happy, considering I had sex with both of them without ever asking either of them to stop. Sex makes men happy, right? Not Drake. Nothing does.

"Why aren't you eating lasagna or bread?"

I swallow hard and shake my head, trying to clear my negative thoughts. "I'm not hungry."

And then my stomach betrays me, gurgling loudly, causing me to cringe with embarrassment.

Chapter Six

DRAKE

"Bullshit," I say, while grabbing the spatula and placing a piece of lasagna on her plate. I don't know why she isn't eating, but that will not fly.

"Drake," she whimpers while pleading with her eyes. She wants me to drop this, but I'm not fucking going to.

"Tell me why you won't eat, and maybe I'll let it go."

She argues again, "I am eating."

I slam my fist on the table, causing her to jump. "Dry salad is not fucking eating. Explain yourself."

"I'm trying not to be a fat pig."

I run a hand through my short hair, wishing it was longer because this woman makes me want to pull it out. Trying not to be a fat pig? That's ridiculous. Natalia isn't skinny, but she's not fat either; she's fucking gorgeous. With wide hips, thick thighs, and a tiny waist, she has curves in all the right places. I hate being with a woman who doesn't have flesh to grab onto.

"You aren't fat," Dante says honestly.

She shrugs like it doesn't matter. "I have a twin sister, and she's rail thin. I'm the one who is fat; For Nicole, it comes easily. She never craves carbs the way I do. The salad fills me up without making me gain weight."

I glare at her. "You have two fucking seconds to take a bite of your lasagna, or I'll bend you over the fucking table and spank your bare ass with my belt."

First, pretty little Natalia gasps and then glares at me. "You will not."

Without taking my eyes off her, I say, "Dante."

My brother knows exactly what I'm asking him to do. He rises out of his chair, walks over to her, and lifts her out of her chair while she complains and tries to get free from him. Pushing her down over the table after moving her pathetic salad out of the way, he holds her down while I get up and get my belt. Our girl is about to learn a valuable lesson. If I say I'll do something, then I will.

Once I come back with my belt, I pull the robe apart and move it to the side, exposing her bare ass. It's been a long time since I spanked a woman. I haven't even wanted to for over a decade. I want to spank her. There's something about Natalia. I want to punish her. Make her cry. Make her scream. I need us to fucking own her.

Dante holds her wrists above her head while she fights him. His palm is pushing her back down while I stare at her beautiful ass. He glances over his shoulder at me, "If you need me to," but I cut him off by shaking my head, "I'm good."

My brother isn't the only one with negative experiences with women. A decade ago, I thought I fell for a woman. Like my brother Damian, I go for submissive women, but not in a BDSM, sir kind of way. I sure as hell don't give a fuck about safe words the way he does. While I've never raped a woman, consent is not always wholly required either. Such is the case right now, as Natalia begs me not to whip her ass with my belt. If I've learned anything about her body in the last couple of hours, she'll like it. It'll hurt. Really fucking hurt, but I think it'll also get her off.

I run my hand across her ass and squeeze her flesh. "Every time I hear you call yourself a fat pig, you will be punished."

Her head is to the side of the table, looking in the other direction, so I can't see her face, but I can hear the anger in her tone. "You will never see me again."

I chuckle loudly and smack her ass with my hand. "If that's the case, I better make it good."

She's never going to see me again? Fucking wrong. While we haven't figured out the logistics yet, she will be ours whether it's what she wants. I fold over my belt, swing it out, and then hit her ass with it, causing her to yelp.

"I hate you both," she bites, but I only respond with a chuckle before striking her sweet skin again. Her ass is already red and looks fucking phenomenal. I hit her again, and she cried out in pain. I rub my hand over the red marks, and she moans loudly.

"I bet you're wet, aren't you, Pretty Girl?"

Her body trembles with her sobs as she pleads with me, "Please, do it again."

This is not the reaction I expected. I thought she'd end up enjoying it, but I didn't know she'd ask for more. I've never had a woman ask for me to hit them more when I've finished.

"Please, Drake, please. I need it."

Dante leans over her back and kisses her tears away while I give her three more lashes on her other cheek. I throw the belt on the floor behind me and force her legs open, pull my pants down, releasing my dick, and slide into her drenched pussy.

"Make it hurt," she whimpers.

Fuck. Despite my assumptions, I had no clue about what I was getting into with this woman. I know I'm in trouble now because she will let me do anything I want to her and enjoy it. I don't fall in love; my black heart won't allow it, but fuck, if she can give me this, I know I'll give her anything she wants.

I press my fingers into where I hit her, and she screams out in a mix of pleasure and pain. Pulling out of her, I order her to turn over. I want to see her face while I fuck her sore body.

Dante pulls her up; she does as she was instructed and yelps in pain when her ass hits the table. I push her legs back, and Dante grabs her ankles as I take in her beautiful body. "Such a pretty fucking pussy."

My dirty praise causes her cheeks to heat. "You like that, don't you, Pretty Girl?"

She drags her fingers up my arms, then over to my chest, and digs her nails into my skin. "Yes, you fucking psycho, I like it, alright?"

Natalia gapes at me with shock when I slap her pussy. I do it five times, listening to her moan as she attempts to buck her hips, but she can't move much with Dante holding her ankles beside her ears. I grin at her while lining up my cock with her entrance. "Next time, I'll use a belt. And I promise you, there will be a next time because I haven't had my fill of this cunt."

Gripping her thighs, I push inside her; she moans loudly as I fuck her. She looks away from me like it's painful to look at me.

"Pretty Girl, look at me."

She turns her head, and her lashes flutter as she lifts her gaze to mine. Those fucking eyes of hers do things to me that I don't care to think about right now. The unshed tears fall as she whispers, "I don't like this position with all my fat on display."

"What did I tell you?"

I pull back and slam back into her, "You. Are. Not. Fucking. Fat." I thrust with every word, trying to drive home the truth to her.

"Who told you that you're fat?"

Dante stands holding her ankles while his eyes dart between us with the same curiosity burning behind his gaze. Her lips form a tight line as she shakes her head, refusing to answer my question. I reach down and wrap my hand around her throat, "If you have nothing to say, you don't need your breath."

Her eyes widen, her arms flail as she fights for air. And Jesus, it's fucking beautiful.

Chapter Seven

NATALIA

The panic sets in even though I can breathe through my nose, and I struggle underneath Drake. I keep expecting Dante to help me, but he doesn't; he continues to hold me in this fucked up pretzel position. When he reaches forward with his other hand and plugs my nose, I freak out, whimpering as much as I can, wriggling my body as I attempt to get free, unsuccessfully, as he continues to move inside me.

White spots form behind my eyes as dizziness sets in. He's going to kill me, and there's nothing I can do about it. Tears stream down my face as the darkness comes for me when he releases both of his hands from me, and I cough and gasp for breath.

"Fucking asshole," I bite when I breathe somewhat normally.

He chuckles loudly, "Always Pretty Girl. Now, let's try this again. Who said you are fat?"

My first instinct is not to tell him because I don't want to let him bully me, but I don't want him to cut off my breath again, so I give in, "My sister."

Drake lifts an eyebrow as he glances at Dante and then continues fucking me. He pulls back and thrusts back into me while he groans. I don't want to enjoy it because I'm pissed at him. My body reacts to the way he hits the perfect spot deep inside me. Dante releases my legs, and I wrap them around Drake's waist, trying to pull him closer. I need more of him. Leaning over me, he places a hand on either side of me on the table and kisses me while he pummels my pussy.

When he kisses my neck tenderly, I am confused because I wouldn't have imagined he could be sweet.

"You are not fat, Pretty Girl. You're perfect."

Again, the internal voice my sister has given me shouts at me, *'If he saw her, he'd change his mind.'*

He lifts himself, grabs my hips, while Dante sucks on my nipples and then bites down, causing me to unravel.

"Harder," I cry.

"Give it to her," Drake says, "Our little pain slut needs it."

Dante bites down so hard I'm sure he's drawn blood, but it sends me into a powerful orgasm that causes me to pulsate around Drake, and he groans loudly as we both come at the same time. He pulls out of me and lifts me off the table, fixing the robe, so I'm covered. He says, "Please be a good girl and eat. I know you're exhausted, but food first and then bed."

"I'll eat because I'm sore. Very sore."

Drake smirks, as if he's pleased with himself. I sit down, move my plate in front of me, and take a bite of the now cold but still delicious lasagna. Sitting silently chewing my food, they both watch

40

me with bizarre interest, and Drake blurts out, "If your sister is a problem, we can take care of it."

I drop my fork and gaze at him. "Take care of it, how?"

He shrugs like it's no big deal and says, "Eliminate her. Kill her. She sounds vile."

I shake my head at him as I pick up my fork and finish eating. "You really are a psychopath. She doesn't like me. I don't know why, but I don't want you to kill her. I love my sister even though she doesn't love me. So no, I don't want you to hurt her."

Drake leans forward, glaring at me with his elbows on the table. "Call me a psychopath again, and you won't get the sleep you desperately need. If you think your cunt is sore now, just wait, Pretty Girl. You won't be able to sit down for a goddamn week."

I look at him sweetly, "Yes, psycho," and snicker.

He goes to rise from his chair but grabs her arm. "Drake. Another time, she's fucking exhausted and probably delirious."

I grin at Drake, feeling like I've won for the moment.

Natalia 1. Drake 0.

Dante walks over to me, pulls my chair out from the table, and bends down, lifting me into his arms.

I wrap my arms around his neck and look into his face. "I can go home."

He stops walking momentarily, kisses me on the forehead, and says, "You're staying here tonight. Where you belong."

Laying my head against his shoulder, I don't argue because I am exhausted.

41

DANTE

I don't even reach the bedroom before she falls asleep in my arms. Laying her down in the middle of the bed, she looks like a goddamn angel. Her dark hair is splayed around the pillow, her lashes flutter slightly, lips parted as she breathes deeply, and I know it will gut me to let her leave in the morning unless I don't.

After undressing, I climb into bed beside her and smile when she turns from her back to her side and wraps her arm around my waist. I lay with her, staring at her, remembering what happened the last time I felt something close to this strong for a woman. Jewel Aiello nearly cost me everything.

I walk into my house after a long and bloody day. We have guys to do our dirty work, but frequently we do it ourselves because there's no fun in delegating. Spending my time carving into the skin of a man who tried to fuck us over is not a bad day. Some people outside in the real world would call me a bad guy, unhinged even, but I never kill someone without a valid reason. I'm not delusional enough to believe that makes me a good man, but there are worse. Far worse.

I glance down at my phone when I get a text message. I'm expecting Jewel to show up at any minute, but I have a message from her.

Help. Kidnapped.

Instantly, I pull up her tracking and find out the Aiellos are holding her at one of their many warehouses. Fuck. Why did they take her? Immediately, I spring into action by contacting Domenic and, of course, he agrees to help because that's what family does.

Drake comes into the bedroom, snapping me out of my terrible memories. If I were sleeping, it'd be a nightmare, but I don't know what you call it when you're awake. Flashback? Maybe because that night most definitely traumatized me.

My brother knows me well and stops at the foot of the bed, shaking his head. He speaks low, probably, so he doesn't wake Natalia up, "It wasn't your fault, man. None of us knew the Aiellos had a daughter they were hiding. You were set up."

I sigh audibly. "Yeah, I know, but our entire family could've died that night."

He raises an eyebrow, letting me know he's done with this conversation, "But we didn't."

I nod as he gets into bed on the other side of Natalia and places his arm just above her ass while mine is around her upper back. Her face is pressed into the crook of my neck, her soft breath fluttering against my skin, her tits pushed against my chest, and of course, my cock is hard as a rock, but I will not wake her up. I'll let her get the rest she needs and fuck her again in the morning the minute she opens those pretty eyes.

Chapter Eight

DRAKE

I sleep a little. If I get three hours of sleep, it's nearly miraculous. With Natalia's soft, warm body between us, I slept like a rock until I felt the jab of my fucking brother's dick against mine. I jump out of bed quickly, instantly seeing red.

"What the fuck is wrong with you?" Dante asks while rubbing sleep from his eyes.

Glaring daggers at him, it takes all the strength I have not to punch my brother in the fucking face. "Your dick on mine is not my favorite way to wake up."

He chuckles as he sits up. "It's not like I was fucking you, asshole. Where's Natalia?"

Good fucking question. All the ways I could punish her for this rude wake-up run through my mind. I shrug. "I don't know, but when I find her, I'm spanking her ass."

My brother climbs out of bed, and we both grab a pair of sweatpants before we go to look for Natalia, but of course, she isn't fucking here.

"We should've tied her ass to the bed."

Why didn't we? The fucking restraints were attached to the bed, ready and waiting for her. Yet, we didn't use them.

Standing in the entryway, we both glared at the door like it should've prevented our little toy from leaving.

"And then what?" Dante asks.

We aren't used to wanting something and not getting it. As De Luca's, we take what we want, but this situation is different because of Domenic and Damian. We're both aware that we can't just keep her without consequences. So we're back to fucking watching her.

DANTE

We have spent the last two weeks working and watching our sweet Natalia from afar. Anywhere she goes, one of us has eyes on her. There have been no dates.

Good girl.

If there had been, they'd be dead. Is that a little over the top? Probably. It doesn't matter though. She's ours, whether or not she realizes it yet. When she walks into Domenic's house for our family dinner, I am relieved to have her in the same house as us, and then I see red when I spot the dried tears on her face.

"Who did this to you?" I ask as I take her face in my hands.

She backs away from me like it's offensive that I'd even touch her. "I'm fine."

My hands drop away, but I keep staring at her, and I want to know who made her cry, "What happened?"

Natalia stands before me with her hands on her hips and shakes her head. "It's nothing. It's just a fight with my sister, so stand down, Cujo."

She walks around me and runs to Giada. I've been dismissed, and I don't fucking like it. I walk to Domenic's office, where the four of us have been instructed to attend a meeting before dinner. When I step into the room, Drake and Damian sit on the black leather couch on one side, and I sit in a matching leather chair opposite Domenic's desk. I try to focus on the meeting, but of course, I can't stop thinking about her.

Chapter Nine

DANTE

I'm not affected by women crying, but seeing Natalia upset twisted something in my chest. I don't like it one bit. When she said it was her sister, it piqued my curiosity. What could her twin have done to her? My beautiful girl asked if I'd kill him had it been a man. Without a fucking doubt, the answer was a resounding yes. It made me wonder if she knew the truth about what I'd done in her honor.

"Dante," Domenic growls, snapping me out of my thoughts. I glance up at him. "Are your men in place?"

I nod as I cross my arms over my chest. "I said they were, and they are. Georgio will be there to receive the shipment."

Four other families are rivals: the Bonettis, Lombardis, Rossis, and the Aiellos. The Bianchis made five. However, they were eliminated. That happens when you target a De Luca, any or all of us. Fuck around and find out. They found out. Although it wasn't us who took Wolf out, if it had been, he would've gotten a lot worse than a couple of bullet holes to end his miserable life. After what he did to my brother, Damian, I would've gladly tortured him for weeks on end. Unfortunately, he got the easy way out, and I never got my chance. There's always another enemy trying to take us out. Three days ago, the Aiellos intercepted our shipment. When a rival family pulls that kind of shit, it's seen as an act of war, plain and simple. They took our product and killed six of our men. That shit won't stand. That's why we were all called here today to handle it. We have another shipment coming in and need to be sure the same thing doesn't happen again. Domenic wants to deal with the Aiello's appropriately, which simply means ending them.

"I don't think we have to worry about them coming after this shipment," Benji, our intel guy, pipes up from the couch, looking tiny, sitting on the sofa between Damian and Drake. It's almost comical. Next to my brothers, he seems like he's only about four feet tall, which isn't the case. He's of average height, unlike us. Domenic and Damian are over six-foot-five, Drake is six-foot-four, but I'm the shortest at six-foot-three.

Domenic stares at Benji, waiting for his reasoning.

He swallows hard as he meets his gaze and continues, "According to my sources, the entire family has taken their women and children. They are no longer in the country; they are hiding."

Drake chuckles lightly. "Fucking wise choice."

Domenic leans back in his chair, arms crossed over his chest, the anger pouring from him, "What country? I want them found."

Benji says, "Italy."

My brother growls in response, "Fuck. Who is your source?"

"Lucas Bonetti."

I'm not surprised that Lucas is his source because the Bonettis want the Aiellos dead more than anyone. They aren't any better than the Bianchis were. Their way of handling business is to kidnap rival's wives, as well as daughters, and torture them until they get what they want. After the Bianchis nearly killed Giada, they took a page from Enzo's playbook. The Bonettis is a rival family, but I suppose we get along, an alliance of sorts, because we will help each other if needed. We don't fuck with them and they don't fuck with us. Of course, if that were ever to change, we'd retaliate.

Domenic picks up his drink and takes a long pull of his whiskey before setting it down. He's frustrated. My brother likes things to go as planned; he hates nothing more than when something he wants is out of reach. I know the feeling with my Natalia. I want her so fucking wrong I can barely focus on anything else, but she keeps saying no, which is not something I'm used to.

We all know Domenic well. When he's quiet, he's always thinking, so we wait for him to decide how he wants to handle things. Finally, he says, "Alright. I want men in Italy. They have to come out for supplies or have them brought in. I want our best men there watching and waiting. Nobody approaches them without my word. Drake, get a hold of Monte; his team can go. They are the best at staying unnoticed."

He notices me arching an eyebrow, "I want Georgio on shipments here."

I want to tell my brother he is a fucking idiot and that Georgio's men should be in Italy, but I don't because he's in charge. We've come a long way since Jewel Aiello, the biggest fucking mistake of my life. She nearly cost me my brother. If Domenic said we were eliminating the entire Aiello family, I wouldn't be sad. I've been waiting for it and hoping for it. I wanted to go to war with them when my brother was lying in the hospital with a hole in his chest, but I was firmly told that would not happen. Through harsh breaths, Domenic told me we wouldn't make a critical situation worse. I heard him but never understood it. We never allow someone to ambush us like that and look the other way. To this day, I do not know why he made the choice he did. I know there's a reason. My brother does nothing without a cause; I just don't know what it is.

Drake narrows his gaze at Domenic. "Are we done here?"

He nods silently, and all five of us file out of his office. When I approach the kitchen, I overhear Giada and Natalia discussing her dating life.

"I don't get a second date ever. What's wrong with me?"

Drake comes over to me and listens as well. We are both obsessed with one woman, and she won't give us either of the time of day after our one night with her. A little arm twisting may be in order because I fucking need her.

"How many first dates have you had?"

Natalia answers, her voice sounding tight, "Six in the last month. I go out with them one time and never hear back."

Giada giggles, "Maybe stop putting out. You know how guys are."

I poke my head forward slightly to see my beautiful girl; she has a glass of wine in her hand, and her long dark hair hangs to her ass in soft curls. Fuck, she's gorgeous, "I haven't."

My dick twitches at her admission like she hasn't been with anyone other than us because it's as if she knows she's ours. Only ours. I've been obsessed with her for two years, and I'd sell my fucking soul to have her again.

Natalia rises off her chair and approaches us, looking at her feet as she walks. She gasps loudly when she crashes into not only me, but Drake. Her gaze travels from my black shoes up to my eyes before she darts her eyes to my brother.

"Can I get by?" she squeaks, and it's fucking adorable. I move to my left slightly, allowing her to pass. Whenever Natalia is here, this is the way it goes. We watch her, and she knows, yet she seems utterly unaware that both of us have been in her house countless times. Fucking her didn't douse the fire; it only stoked the flames.

Chapter Ten

NATALIA

Mafia men are not good men. Yes, I notice how they stare at me with those heated eyes. I'm aware. Everyone has watched how their eyes track me like a wolf tracks a lamb before sinking teeth into its flesh. The one night I spent with them, having more orgasms than I could count, didn't seem to change their fascination with me. I'm not afraid of these men, even if I should be. I dealt with Gia's father for years, and then that Enzo guy. Thoughts of him still make me physically ill after what he did to her. I giggle at myself as I glance around their bathroom. The shower is massive, with multiple shower heads; the countertop has enough space for four people to live comfortably with black granite. All the faucets are stainless steel. The walls are dark gray other than the one on the far end, which is a lighter color with gray splashes. My gaze darts around the room, taking in what can only be defined as opulence. Whatever problems the De Luca family has, it's not money. But then there's a price for everything. I often wonder what would happen to Giada if Domenic died or ended up with a lengthy prison sentence. I know they have money tucked away to care for their families. If that were to happen still it would break her. They have enemies, they always have, and I worry about her. She'll always be a target and now their child will be as well.

After washing my hands, I head back downstairs to my friend. She stands in the kitchen with Domenic's arms wrapped around her while she giggles as he nuzzles her neck. Am I jealous of this intense love they share? If I'm honest with myself, I am a little. One day, I'll meet a regular guy that wants more than one date.

Domenic releases her when he sees me. I hug her, "I have to go. I need to rehearse a new song I'm putting into my set tomorrow."

She folds her arms across her chest. "You could practice here. We *do* have a piano, you know."

Rolling my eyes at her, I say, "Obviously, I know. I helped you pick it out."

Giada wanted a piano three months ago to ensure her kids were well-rounded. The child isn't born yet, so it's a little putting the cart before the horse but of course, I helped her. I wanted to be sure it was something I'd be happy with because I know that I'll be charged with teaching the kids when the time comes.

"Please," her blue eyes sparkle as she nearly begs, "You know how much I love listening to you play."

It's true. I know how much she loves it and she won't be there tomorrow because Domenic doesn't like her going without him. It's not a control thing, it's more about her safety.

I relent, "Fine. Only for a little while, though."

She claps excitedly, "Yay!"

I walk out to their massive living room, which has floor-to-ceiling windows, a couple of large white sofas, and sitting chairs. The black grand piano fit in perfectly, like the space was designed for it.

Sitting down in front of the piano, I take a deep breath to calm my emotions as Giada yells, "Everyone, the amazing Natalia Grant!"

I roll my eyes at her and ignore the clapping from the De Luca brothers as I press the keys for the first few notes. My fingers glide over the keys as I sing the haunting melody. I'm a pianist; usually, you don't expect a pianist to sing, but I've started only in the last few years. When I first incorporated it into my show, I was nervous people wouldn't like it. However, I was pleased that they enjoyed it and it added an element that other performers didn't have. Ticket sales increased and videos started popping up on YouTube. It's not ballet, but it feeds my need to create.

Drake and Dante watch me like hawks, never taking their eyes from me, their gazes traveling my body with a heat that makes me feel like I can feel their fingers on my skin. Domenic holds Giada in his arms as she sways back and forth, his hands planted firmly on her bump. The room is thick with emotion as I sing about wanting, essentially what she has, something solid, something real. It's a song of intense longing and the theme of my life. Doesn't everybody want to be loved? The piano is the only love I've ever known. I finish playing, *Unloveable*, to the small crowd and spot Giada with tears running down her face as she claps. God, I love her. I know I may never have a man that loves me the way Domenic loves her, but I'll always have Gia. Her and music. Those are the two constants in my life. For now, it has to be enough. I'd rather dance, but that was taken from me.

Just for my friend, I break into my little rendition of *You are My Sunshine*, because I know she sings this for the baby all the time. She places her hand over her enormous belly and sings along, knowing I'm playing this for her. After playing for three hours, I stand and stretch. "I have to go, Gia."

She walks over and hugs me. "Thank you," she whispers into my hair. I hug her back, "Anytime queen," and she giggles.

I wave goodbye to everyone else as she walks me to the door. As she walks me to my car, she asks, "Are you okay?"

Laughing I say, "Oh just fine. There might be a little too much testosterone in your house, though."

She sighs audibly. "You aren't wrong. It's practically a testosterone factory."

We share a few laughs while Domenic stares at us from the doorway. He doesn't like her out of his sight., "I better go before your husband loses his mind."

Sliding into my vehicle as she nods, "Yeah, he thinks if he can't see me, I might disappear."

I roll down my window and close the door. "It wouldn't be the first time. You can't blame him for his concern."

Leaning down, she kisses my cheek. "I love you, Nat. Good luck tomorrow. Break a leg and all that."

"Love you too," I call after her as she joins her husband in the doorway and I drive around their circular driveway to make my way home.

The traffic is heavy, it always seems to be between our houses. It's not far, but the massive amount of vehicles on the road always makes it seem further than it is. People lay on their horns as if it'll make people move faster when there's nowhere to go. I wait patiently for my chance to turn onto the street I live on. I'll never understand the hustle and bustle here. It seems people are always in such a hurry, but I'm not like that at all. I don't like getting upset about things I can't control. It seems pointless to get wound up about things you can't change.

I pull into the underground parking for my penthouse and drive into a spot near the elevators. Many people would love living in a place like this, but I don't. I want a house with space to plant flowers. And independence from my parents that have no use for me. I do not know why they even pay for my home. I want them to never speak to me again. No, that's a complete lie. I want them to love me like they do her. *Nicole.* They say jealousy is toxic, but how could I feel any differently? She has everything I've ever wanted. My sister is gorgeous, has a legion of faithful friends that follow her around like their fans, and the undying love of my parents. In their eyes, Nicole does no wrong. She's as vicious as a rattlesnake. Still, they keep their rose-colored glasses on and worship her as she sits on top of the pedestal they've put her on since the day she was born, leaving me to wonder the same thing I've wondered a million times. *What's wrong with me? Why am I so unlovable?*

Chapter Eleven

DRAKE

The De Luca brothers have our hands in nearly everything illegal, except for human trafficking and prostitution. That's where my brother Domenic draws the line. We rarely hurt women and we never lay a hand on children. I don't agree on not hurting women because sometimes there's a need for it, but with kids, I agree. They are always off limits for us.

One of our largest sources of revenue is drugs, and you'd think people wouldn't dream of fucking us over, but they do. There's an excellent reason we don't touch the shit. Drugs make you stupid, kids. Really fucking stupid. And desperate. Heroin specifically in the current case. One hit and you're done. Addicted. An absolute slave to the madness that it makes you crave. People know this, yet they inject that needle into their veins for the first time and then their lives as they know it are over. They will do anything to score more. Very few people can afford to have a heroin habit. Even those that can eventually cannot maintain it. Every day, their body needs more as they chase that elusive high. The problem is once you're addicted to it, it's no longer just about the high you'll never achieve again. It's the sickness.

I'm told the inability to sleep for days at a time, the bone pain, and muscle cramps are the worst of it. However, the sweating, high blood pressure, racing heart, watery discharge from the eyes and nose, nausea, vomiting and diarrhea don't sound like a day at the park either. Like I said, they get desperate and make poor choices in the pursuit of the drug that now rules their lives.

When one of our guys in distribution told me he had been robbed of his entire supply, I was slightly surprised because he's been a solid worker for the last six years. He sat an interrogation with both Dante and myself for twelve hours because we don't take anyone at their word. We were both concerned he might be lying and either using drugs or attempting to steal money from us. Both of which are terrible decisions. Of course, the story began with a woman, a pretty blonde. It always starts with a woman or ends with one. However, when he informed us that the woman was none other than Nicole Grant, our ears perked up with delight. After a little digging, we confirmed that this woman is indeed Nicole, who is the twin sister of our little obsession. So we brought her in, not willingly, of course.

Nicole sits on her knees with her hands tied behind her back. Normally, a sight like that would make my dick hard, but not this time. Some men might find the thin blonde type attractive, but I prefer women like Natalia, with meat on their bones. I want flesh to dig my fingers into while I fuck them. However, apparently Marcus does not agree because that's how she got him. She used her body to get into his house, and then robbed him while he slept. We will deal with him. There will be no mercy for allowing this to happen, but right now I'm focused on Nicole and how we can turn this to our benefit.

Her blonde hair is drenched with sweat as shivers, "I'm so-so-rry," she whimpers loudly.

I rub my hand across my jaw. "Tell me about your sister."

Her blue eyes snap to mine, widening, as her mouth falls open, and she blinks several times like she's trying to process my words, "What about her?"

Dante looms over her, an expression of intrigue on his face. "Tell us everything."

"And then you'll let me go?" She asks hopefully as I chuckle, "You'll tell us everything or you'll die slowly. Painfully."

Nicole's eyes water, and I'm not sure if it's from the withdrawal or if she's going to cry. It doesn't actually matter because the only reason she's still alive is because we want information from her. She doesn't know it yet, but her sister is the only thing keeping her alive at the moment.

"There isn't much to tell. She's the fat one, the ugly duckling. Nobody likes her, not me, not my parents. No one."

Dante balls his fists, and pulls his leg back and kicks her in the face with enough force to knock her teeth out, but she turns her head in time to avoid losing any. She cries out in pain as his foot connects with the side of her face, and her head smacks into the wall behind her.

"Dante," I growled, "Stand back. You'll get your chance."

He inhales a sharp breath as he turns and glares at me. I nod, and he steps back from her reluctantly. We both have a fascination with our sweet Natalia, but his differs from mine. I want to fuck her and make her cry, but I think my brother is in love with her. He wants to protect her and do all the romantic shit. It's the only reason we haven't taken her yet, because we are not on the same page. I expect that to change because the youngest De Luca brother is getting twitchy with his need for her. Eventually, he'll snap and agree.

"Why don't your parents like her?"

I get sibling rivalry, but why her parents wouldn't like her is beyond me. Natalia has a bubbly, sweet personality and I can't imagine anyone not liking her. Every family has drama, but I can't imagine how she would be at the center of it.

She grins at me like she's holding the world's biggest secret and shakes her head. "Nope. You're going to kill me, anyway. I'll take this one to the grave."

Dante reacts emotionally, while I'm always calm and calculated. An emotional response is dangerous because if I let him, he'd kill her and we'd never get what we both want. I know it's his need to protect Natalia that's driving it. Still, keep your eye on the prize and all that.

Pulling out my cell phone, I call T, "Bring it."

Physical violence isn't how you get a junkie to talk. Only one thing will, the drugs they desire more than their next breath.

"Dante, untie her."

Glaring at her, I stand back, my hands in my pockets, "Don't try anything stupid. I'll give you what you want and then you'll give us what we want or there'll be no more. Understood?"

She nods emphatically. "Yes. Oh God, thank you."

T walks in and I nod to him, "Give it to her. She knows what to do."

He walks over to her and hands her the syringe with the heroin, ready to go, and quickly searches for a vein with shaky hands and injects it into her arm. She hands the syringe to Dante, and he walks away to toss it in a bottle and seal it. It's not perfect but we don't have a sharps container because normally there's no drug use here.

"Now. Start talking before I unleash my brother on you."

She nods as she takes in a shaky breath. "We don't have the same father."

I tilt my head curiously as I cock an eyebrow at her. "Twins can't have different fathers."

Okay, it's possible, I suppose. We all saw the news report about the woman who had fraternal twins by two different men, but I'm sure that's not what we are dealing with here. That has to be a rare situation—one that's not likely to happen again. What are the odds? A million to one, I don't actually know, but it's got to be something like that.

Chapter Twelve

NATALIA

Gia and I used to go out drinking but her life is different now. She isn't able to drink, since she's pregnant and Domenic doesn't like her hanging out in bars. I don't know that I'd say he's controlling, more protective. He lets her do whatever she wants, with security, of course, but she doesn't like to cause him stress. And how fun is it to go hang out among drunk people when you have to stay sober? Still, I want to spend time with my bestie before she's a mom and has to devote all her time to a crying, pooping newborn. When she texted me declaring a pool day, I couldn't refuse.

Domenic stands watching from inside the French doors as Gia waddles over to me in a black bikini, and a protruding belly which she always has a hand on. The love she has for this baby before they're even born is heartwarming. The way her husband stares at her like she's his entire world causes my chest to clench with slight jealousy. I want that. Desperately. I'm happy for her, but I wish I could have something real the way they do. Not a mafia man, of course, but someone that looks at me like I hung the damn moon.

She turns to him, places her hands on her hips, "Dom."

"Bellissima."

She giggles with a shake of her head. "Go to work."

His gaze drops to her belly, and he says, "I'll be in my office here. I already told you I'm not leaving until the baby is born."

Turning to me, she rolls her eyes. As he walks away, I assume to his office.

"He's going to drive me crazy for the next six weeks, Nat. The constant hovering gets to be a little much. Domenic stands around like he's waiting for some kind of tragedy to happen."

"Rough life," I quip as she lowers herself onto a lounge chair.

She lies back with her hands folded over her stomach. "One day, Nat. Whoever you're meant to be with will find you, and he will know what I do."

I laugh loudly, "Until he sees Nicole, right? That's how it happens every single time. If a man has a chance with Nicole, he's over me in a flash."

"Look at me," she says, so I do, turning to her in my chair, "The right man will never look at her because he won't be able to see anyone other than you."

Throughout school, whenever I had a boyfriend, Nicole would snatch him away from me. It became more predictable as the years went on. She would sleep with them, and then she was done. It always felt to me like she wasn't even interested in them. She only wanted to hurt me. And she did. Repeatedly. I have gone on so many first dates recently and then just gotten ghosted and I've wondered if she was involved. How could she be? She doesn't know about the dates. We don't live together anymore. She'd have to be stalking me, and I don't think even Nicole would go that far. Clearly, they're just not that into me. The story of my life.

She raises her eyebrow with a devilish grin. "You know... Dante would give his left arm to go out with you. He'd never give her the time of day. *And* he wouldn't ghost you."

I firmly shake my head, showing a definite "No. I'm glad you're happy, but that's not the life I want. I will never be with Dante."

Gia tilts her head at me with obvious disapproval. "He is the sweetest out of all four of them."

I laugh, "And we both know he kills people. Does whatever with drugs. He is a criminal, Gia. I know that doesn't matter to you, but it does for me."

Rolling her eyes at me, she asks, "Speaking of evil. How are things with Nicole?"

For years, Giada has tried to convince me to finally rid myself of my sister. Sometimes, we do things we know aren't good for us. Every week I go to our family dinners that kill me slowly. On top of that, I try to develop a relationship with her. Once a month, I convince her to spend time with me, knowing the very reason she agrees. It's not because she wants to see her sister. I'm her punching bag. For the mere chance she might decide I'm not as worthless as she constantly says I am, I set myself up for the abuse. It always goes the same. We meet for lunch or dinner; she makes comments about my choice of food, finds some way to remind me I'm not like her, too fat, ugly and that I'll always be alone. Being around my sister is like pouring salt into an oozing wound. Yet, my need for love and acceptance from my family means I'll willingly put myself through it time and time again. Do I know that it's all incredibly toxic for me? Yes. Knowing something is wrong and being able to stop it are two very different things. Old habits die hard.

"The same as they always are."

My sister is an uncomfortable subject that I'd rather not talk about. Giada doesn't understand why I haven't cut her out of my life entirely. She can't understand why I still have hope that one day Nicole will wake up and realize how terrible she's been to me.

My best friend looks at me with pain in her eyes. I know her next words before she says them.

"Have you been cutting?"

Giada is the only person in this world that knows about my dirty little secret. She doesn't understand my way of dealing with the pain. It's not like I do it every day, I don't. Sometimes it's several months between cutting episodes. Some people numb emotional pain with drugs or alcohol. The razor blade is my drug of choice, I suppose.

"No," I lie, because it's what she needs to hear. Do I enjoy lying to her? No, of course, I don't, but she doesn't need the added stress with her baby due soon. She needs rest and relaxation, not to be overcome with worry about something she can't change.

"Good," she smiles at me. "Do you want to help a beached whale off this chair so I can go in the pool?"

Rising to my feet, I stretch out my hand to help her up. She stands on her feet with a grunt. "I want this child out. I'm over this."

We walk over to the pool and step into the warm water and she sighs audibly, "This is the only time this baby doesn't kick me relentlessly."

She has had a difficult pregnancy. The baby moves nonstop, making it hard for her to even sleep. A few months ago, she had to sleep in a chair because every time she lies down; the baby gets rambunctious. This after months of terrible nausea that she hid from everyone, including me. Domenic was the only one that knew she was pregnant until things settled for Damian. He was in a terrible place and his brother worried that sharing their good news would only make things worse for him. Who says a lethal man can't have a heart?

Chapter Thirteen

DRAKE

She tosses her head back with a smile on her face. "Fuck yeah."

"Who is Natalia's father?"

With an evil grin, she says, "Why do you care?"

I shrug, pretending I care far less than I do. "Just wondering."

She sits on the cold concrete, her eyes lighting up with excitement. "Let me go, give me a brick, and I'll sing like a bird."

I step over to her, and squat in front of her, my face less than an inch from hers, "You aren't the pretty one, dead girl. My brother and I will fight over you, though. We'll both be so fucking hard at the thought of ending your miserable existence. The only brick you'll get is the ones tied to your arms and legs to weigh your dead body down in whatever body of water we decide will be your last resting place."

She trembles with the fear that I love so much as I grip her chin and tilt her head back. "I'll fuck you both. I just need more."

I shake my head before I grin at her. "You'd let both my brother and I use you like the disgusting whore you are? Is that what you're offering?"

Tears well in her eyes, and her confidence now appears to be completely gone. "Yes," she whimpers, "Anything you want."

I sigh as I shake my head, "No thanks, dead girl. We don't fuck garbage."

Dante watches us with blood thirst. I know my brother and his obsession with Natalia. He wants to end this bitch's life as much as I do, but he also knows it's not an option right now.

"You're going to kill me," she says, as if she's just now realizing it. A little slow.

I nod at her, "Probably dead, girl. When? How? That depends on your sister. Do you think she'd trade her life for yours?"

"No," she whimpers loudly, "She won't."

Rising to my feet, I tell her the truth, "You won't get more until you give us what we want, dead girl."

We do not know why Natalia's family appears to dislike her so much. Whatever it is, none of our guys have been able to uncover it. What we found, however, is alarming. Between the ages of fourteen to sixteen, she was admitted to a psychiatric facility four times. There were no reports of abuse. The hospital stays began after a surgery on both knees after a traumatic injury. An injury that makes no fucking sense to me or Dante. How is it possible that she was dancing, and fell, shattering both knees? It's what her medical records say, but it's nonsense. It has to be. She fell from the floor to her knees and caused that kind of damage? Bullshit.

We walk out of the room and I nod to T, "Chain her up. I don't want her to move."

"Yes, Boss. Is she-?"

I chuckle, "Off limits? No. As long as she lives, you can have a little fun."

Damian and Domenic would have a conniption if they heard me say that. This warehouse is behind the hotel we own. Nobody knows what we do here. Other than Dante, my family thinks we store extra supplies in there, which we do. We have a family business, but this hotel and this warehouse are businesses that only Dante and I run.

Will we really kill Natalia's junkie sister? If we don't get what we want, yes, we'll end her pathetic existence without a second thought. I don't get some perverse pleasure from killing women, but I also don't think they're off limits because they were born with a pussy. If you piss me off, I will kill you. It's very simple. Children are the only ones I probably wouldn't be able to hurt. Luckily, I've never been presented with that situation.

We walk out to my truck, silent. Both of us know better than to risk anyone overhearing us. When we both get inside and I pull out my parking spot, Dante asks, "So we will not kill her?"

I chuckle as I put the truck into drive. "Patience, little brother. That bitch is going to give us exactly what we both want."

Of course, Dante doesn't bother asking where we're going because he knows as well as I do. The tracker in her car alerted us both that she's at Domenic's house. She could already be chained to a bed in the home we share. But that's too risky. Within weeks and maybe even days, my sister-in-law would freak out about her best friend being missing. Domenic would get involved immediately because he can't have Bellissima upset. He's always been overprotective of Giada, but since she's been pregnant with his child, it's only increased. My brother would turn the world upside down, looking for Natalia to appease his wife. If he's paid any attention at all, we would be suspects one and two. Domenic doesn't know we've been in her house, or that we installed cameras, trackers on her phone, but we both are aware that he's seen us watching her. Domenic has a talent most people don't even know about. He is quiet, and it may seem as if he's not paying attention, but he is. He always is. There isn't a single glance that's gone unnoticed by him if he's in the room. We haven't been secretive. And fucking Dante has asked her out more times than I can count.

The plan has always been to take her. Damn the consequences. However, now things have lined up beautifully and that won't be necessary. My brother and I have different goals, but that's okay if we both get what we want. He wants to love her. Dante is banking on her one day, returning his feelings. Maybe she will. Maybe she won't. He believes in love. I don't. The last time my idiot younger brother loved a woman, we all almost died.

I don't want her heart. I want the fear in her eyes, the orgasms that she'll try to resist, the fight, the struggle, and even her breath.

Imagining her gasping, fighting for air, that's the shit that gets my dick hard. *Pretty little sunshine.*

Turning on the side street, Dante groans, "I'm tiring of waiting. I just want to take her."

I shake my head as I approach Domenic's gated house. "Exercise a little fucking control. You don't think with your head. That's how Jewel almost ended the entire family. Just because we can't take her doesn't mean we can't have a little fun."

NATALIA

I feel their eyes on me before I can even see them. Over the past few months, it seems like they show up whenever I'm here. It's unnerving and exciting all at once. These men are dangerous and I shouldn't like the attention. I'll never give either of them the time of day, but it feels good to be noticed. I'm not used to it like Nicole is. *If they saw her, they'd be looking at her instead.*

"I'm going to go to the bathroom and get changed. Will you be okay?"

Giada giggles while splashing in the pool. "I'll be fine. Sitting down isn't nearly as hard as getting up."

Placing my hand on her stomach, I look up at her. "Gia, I'm thrilled for you. You're going to be an amazing mom."

The sobs are immediate, intense, and I do not know what I did. However, in under three minutes papa bear comes growling toward the pool, "What did you do?"

Domenic grabs a towel and holds it out for her as she steps out of the pool, still crying. He wraps her up and pulls her into his chest. "Hormones," she squeaks out as she wraps her arms around him.

I watch him hold her like she's the only thing in the world that matters to him and feel jealous, which I hate. Jealousy isn't an attractive trait. How can I not? She has everything. I'm not exactly dying to have a baby, but I think I want one someday. Having a husband who would literally do anything to protect you, though? I want that. I take a deep breath and try to think positively. Maybe tomorrow's date will go differently than the others.

Chapter Fourteen

NATALIA

As I stand in their bathroom, I stare at my reflection in this pink bikini Giada convinced me to buy a few months ago. I compare my body to my sisters. I know I shouldn't still I do, it's become a compulsion I can't fight. Her arms are smaller than mine, as are her breasts. Mine are too big, they don't fit with my body. Then nothing looks right when I stare at myself. I've always been heavier than my twin, but now that I don't dance, it's worse. Tears roll down my cheeks as I allow the self hatred to seep in. It's not that I want to feel this way, I don't. There's nothing I wouldn't do to have confidence in my own skin. I fake the smiles. I put on a convincing performance, but it's all an act. It always has been.

The door opens, and my heart slams against my ribcage as the two men I try to avoid step beside me, Drake on my right and Dante on my left. I freeze, my eyes still on the mirror but watching them instead of myself.

Dante grips my chin and turns my face to his. "I'm tired of waiting for you."

"So don't."

He drags his thumb across my bottom lip. "Finally we agree," lowering his head, he presses his lips to mine and I don't fight him. Instead, I part my lips and accept his tongue into my mouth. While he kisses me I feel Drake's gaze burning my skin, then his fingers trail my arms before he places his hand under my chin, breaking my kiss with Dante, and he cups my face with his powerful hands and slams his lips to mine. I should stop this, but I can't think straight. Their scent is overpowering and has me weak in the knees. Dante's kiss was sweet, but Drake's is anything but. He pushes his tongue into my mouth hungrily and moves my head the way he wants it. He pulls back from me with a glare on his face, and hands me my phone.

"If you want to see your sister alive again, you'll be at the address I texted you in an hour."

I turn so I can see both of them. "What? What did you do?"

Dante grins, "Be a good girl, and nobody will get hurt. You will say goodbye to Giada, go home, pack some clothes, and then come to the address Drake sent you."

"What?"

My head is spinning, I do not know what's happening right now, "What?"

Do I know any other words? Right now, I am not sure about anything.

Drake leans into me and kisses the corner of my mouth. "See you soon, Pretty Girl. Do as you're told or she's dead."   ·

"She hates me. My sister would not lift a finger to save me, so why should I?"

Dante smiles, "Because you couldn't be more different from Nicole if you tried. If she were a complete stranger, you'd save her, wouldn't you?"

I swallow the lump in my throat because he's not wrong. I don't know what they know about my family, but I won't let her die. Not even when I know if the roles were reversed, she'd sit and laugh while they killed me.

Drake reaches around and pats my ass. "Tick Tock, Sunshine."

And with that, they both turn and leave.

Jesus, Nicole, what have you done? According to Giada, they don't kill women. Is she wrong? Obviously, her husband doesn't know about this.

My phone chimes with a text message. I glance down at it and see it's from Dante, which is odd because I never put his number in my phone.

> Fifty minutes.

Had you asked me an hour ago, I would've told you that Dante was lethal, yes, but sweet. He's always been kind to me. Caring even. Now though? He's obviously as unhinged as his brother. Fear swirls in my belly as my mind continues to race, but underneath it all is sorrow.

Am I really going to show up at this address to save Nicole? How do they even know her? I have far more questions than I do answers.

> How do I know you actually have her? How do I know she's alive?

I get changed into the clothes I came in while I wait for Dante's response. My phone chimes with his response as I slip on my sandals. Glancing at my phone, it says a picture is downloading.

I swallow hard when I look at the picture of my sister, on her knees, chained to the wall behind her, and dried tears on her cheeks. *This is real.* This is as real as it gets. Once Giada apologizes for her crying when I was only being nice to her, I grab my bag and head downstairs to say my goodbyes. Although I reassured her it's okay, I have much bigger issues to deal with. I decide on my way out the door that I'm not going home first to pack a bag. I don't know what they want, but I'm going to find out, and then I'm leaving.

Slipping into my car, I put the address he texted me into my GPS and leave. It's a twenty-minute drive from Giada's house, and that's a relief because I'll be there in under their one hour demand. As I make the drive to the unknown address, I run through the different things my mind thinks they could want. I come up empty because yes; I know Dante has a thing for me. But Drake? That man hates me just for being alive. I have done nothing to him. I've always been pleasant, yet every time I've run into him, he looks at me like he wants to tear me limb from limb. If I've earned his ire, then I don't know what it is.

For a moment, as I pull into the driveway of this mystery home, I wonder if she fucked one of them to end up chained in what looks like a basement, but I dismiss it. This is why you don't get mixed up with men like this. It's the exact reason I've told Dante no every time he's asked me out. My skin tingles with the need to ease the pain. Right now, I can't use the razor blades in my purse, although I always carry them with me. I'm sure they know I've pulled up to their mansion. I assume one of them owns it. Traveling the circular driveway, and park as the gates that were open close behind me, giving me the feeling of being trapped. It feels like walls are closing in on me and I put my car in park and step outside into the cool air. It was warm earlier but now that I'm here it feels cold. I wonder if it's the weather or if these men carry the coldness within them.

I glance around at the neatly trimmed hedges. There are flowers planted all around the front of the house, and it makes it look non-threatening, but somehow, I know better. Danger lurks inside this beautiful building. The outside is a beautiful sandstone, and I can picture a princess being kept here. The only thing missing is the drawbridge with hungry snakes in the water below. I snicker to myself as I realize this castle has snakes. But they're inside, waiting for me.

After taking a deep breath, I step up to the porch and ring the doorbell as I take in the black iron doors with an intricate swirly design. There's no doubt these doors cost more than my car is worth, which is sad, but I will not think about that right now.

It's Dante that opens the door and waves me inside. I step into the foyer and if I weren't so angry that I've been forced to come here for whatever reason, I'd be in awe of this home. I take a quick glance around at the white walls, expensive artwork hanging sporadically. As

I follow Dante, I spot a living room to the left with a white sectional sofa. Off to the right, I notice a large white dining table with matching chairs with black legs. A black iron candelabra sits on the table, but a quick look tells me they've never been lit.

"Have a seat," Drake says from the other side of the room.

I sink down onto the sofa that looks modern and not comfortable, but surprisingly, it's quite cozy. Other than the two men that take a seat across from me on a large matching love seat.

"Do you want a drink?" Dante asks.

I laugh. "This isn't a social call. Tell me what you want."

Drake leans back with a grin, runs his hand over his neatly trimmer beard. "Right to business. I like the way you think, Pretty Girl."

My gaze moves to Dante when he speaks. "Your sister owes us a great debt. One she'd already be dead for if it weren't for you."

I shake my head. "That's impossible. My parents have money. She'd never have to come to you for money."

Drake grins. "You obviously don't know about your sister's little problem. She stole drugs from us. If you give us your cooperation, she will be the first person ever to get away with that.

Did I know my sister used drugs? Yes, recreationally. When she's out at a club, she will partake in ecstasy and whatever else seems like a good idea. But a drug problem? Addicted to the point of stealing from the mafia? No. That is definitely news to me.

Arching a brow, I ask, "And what do you want?"

Drake's lips curl up into a sinister grin, the closest to a smile I've ever seen from him. "You."

I clutch my purse with a white-knuckle grip, like it can somehow save me. I shake my head and say, "I'm not for sale. Goodbye, I'm going home."

Dante glares at me like I've wronged him greatly. "Check your phone."

Reaching into my purse, I retrieve my phone and see a text message from Drake—another number I never put into my phone. Before I press play, I see a house—not just a house, but my house. As the video starts, I watch my home go up in flames.

Chapter Fifteen

DRAKE

Her mouth drops open as her eyes widen as she shrinks before us, "You burned-"

She doesn't finish her sentence because I'm sure this is unbelievable to her. She swallows hard several times, and darts her tongue out, licking her lips before she speaks.

"Why?"

Lifting one shoulder, I tell her honestly, "Insurance."

She shakes her head as if this is confusing, even though it's quite simple. I had her house burned down when I knew she was on her way here. She didn't bother to go home and pack a bag like she was told.

Natalia laughs nervously, "This is insane."

I nod, fully aware of how crazy this is. I'm not an idiot. I know this isn't something most men would do to keep what they want. When I kissed her, it only cemented my obsession. That's grown to the point of consuming me. However, I am not Dante. I don't want her heart. I want the fear in her eyes. The struggle and even her breath. The thought of her trembling and gasping for air makes my dick twitch.

"You burned down my home. Do you know how many people could've died?"

Drake chuckles darkly. "Sweet little Sunshine, any lives lost are inconsequential. It got you here, and that's all that matters. We didn't kidnap you. You came with us on your own."

Tears well in her eyes. "I did not come here on my own. I was coerced."

Dante nods in agreement. "You were, but you're free to go if you don't want to be here. That means your sister will be handled, as all our problems are."

A tear runs down her cheek and I fight the urge to get up and lick it from her skin. "You'll murder her."

I answer while she stares at my brother in disbelief. "Yes. And unfortunately, we'll have to inform your parents that you chose not to save Nicole."

She puts her face in her hands and sobs and it twists something in my chest, but not enough to change my mind. We watch her silently as she cries but then, like a faucet, it's turned off as she looks up at us with pure hatred, "Fine. Set her free and you can have whatever it is you want from me."

Again, my dick twitches with need for her. Her mouth, cunt, and even that sexy little ass. I fucking want all of her.

I rise from my spot on the loveseat and walk over to her. Taking a seat beside her, I take her face in my hands. "Now we own you. The word no means nothing to us. Scream for us to stop. We never will. You're ours. There's no going back."

Sliding my hand from her face to her neck, I feel her pulse racing under my fingertips. And it's so fucking beautiful. Her fear makes me insane with desire.

"For how long?"

Dante comes and sits on the other side of her as I growl, "Until we are both done with you."

"I want my sister set free right now."

My brother speaks low into her ear, but loud enough that I can hear him, "I'll make the call, but as long as you understand if you run, we will find her and kill her. You won't get this chance to save her again."

Her glare stays focused on me without wavering. She says, "Make the fucking call."

While Dante places the call, I run the pad of my thumb over her lips before pushing the digit into her mouth, "Suck."

My dick begins to fucking weep as she obeys me and sucks it like it's a fucking cock. Her tongue swirls around the tip, causing me to groan. Fuck. If she sucks dick like that, I'm going to be in her throat constantly.

I retract my thumb as Dante ends the call. "There. It's done. Your sister will be home shortly."

Again Natalia flashes me a death glare, "Just so we're clear, I fucking hate you both. I hope you both tire of this sinister game quickly, because the thought of either of you being inside of me makes me nauseous."

I grin, "You'll hate fucking us until you love us, hate fucking you, Pretty Girl."

NATALIA

I knew they weren't good men, but this was beyond my wildest nightmares. Drake groans as he takes my hand, stands and pulls me up so I'm standing between him and his brother. "I can't fuck wait to break you, little sunshine."

I have no idea why they call Domenic De Luca the devil when there's no man more evil than his brother Drake. The man is worse than Satan himself. There is nothing good in him, no redeemable qualities. The man is pure evil. When he vowed to break me, I believed him.

He pulls me down a long hallway and into a large bedroom. I glance around the room as I stand frozen. The walls are a dark gray in contrast to how it looked in the living room. But it's the bed that makes me nearly laugh at them both. It's a king-sized bed with a black iron frame, but instead of normal bedposts, the tops have black skulls. Skulls. Even the bed has to say, I'm a threatening bad guy and I wonder whose room this is. Surely, the brothers don't share a bed.

"Whose room is this?"

Drake lifts a shoulder. "Ours now."

I turn to him and arch a brow. "You share a bed with your brother?"

He chuckles, the deep sound rumbling through his chest. "We'll figure out the logistics as we go. One of us will always sleep in here with you. This is new for us, so we'll figure it out."

I glance at Dante. "Have you not done this before?"

Dante answers, "Not exactly. We've shared a woman sexually, but neither of us is accustomed to sleeping with women."

My gaze darts between the two of them as I take in his words, but I'm not really surprised. Both men definitely strike me as fuck it and forget it guys, which is just fine with me. Maybe after a few times, they'll be ready to move on and let me out of this bizarre deal. Nicole to live to further torment me and I can go back to my life as I knew it.

"Clothes off," Drake says, causing my gaze to snap to his. I swallow hard as the nerves set in. "Can you turn the lights off at least?"

Drake grabs the back of his black t-shirt and whips it off. "No. Get fucking undressed. Don't make me remind you of what's at risk."

I fucking hate my sister right now, possibly more than she hates me. This is all her fault. If it weren't for her stupidity, I wouldn't be here getting ready to take my clothes off with all the lights on for two men that are vile human beings.

"Natalia," Drake growls, his menacing glare causes me to shiver as I remove my clothes with trembling fingers.

Dante steps closer to me, brushing his thumbs over the thin fabric of my bra covering my breasts, and kisses me. His lips are soft, his tongue slow and sensual, sliding against mine as a whimper escapes from me. The same one I promised myself they wouldn't get. I don't want to make this enjoyable for either of them. Drake undoes my bra as he stands behind me. Dante drags my straps over my arms and tosses the garment to the floor as his brother spins me so I'm facing him. He cups my breasts in his large hands, "Are you scared, Sunshine?"

"Yes."

He pinches both of my nipples, causing me to yelp with pain and pleasure. "Good. You should be. There will be no safe words. No limits. What we want, we take."

His brother kneels behind me and drags my panties down my legs before spreading my ass cheeks and pressing his face between my trembling legs. "Fuck. This scent is intoxicating."

I jump when I feel his tongue press inside me.

Chapter Sixteen

DANTE

How is it possible that she tastes even better than the first time I tasted her? I swirl my tongue around the inside of her pussy and she moans even though I know she doesn't want to enjoy this. Right now she hates us both, but I know in time that will change. One day soon she'll be begging for us to make her come.

Drake pulls her delicious body away from me and lifts her into his arms, and lays her in the middle of the bed. "Hands and knees," he orders. She looks fucking gorgeous, naked and waiting for us, even as she trembles with fear.

We both take our pants and underwear off quickly. Neither of us has any interest in delaying this. Both my brother and I have been waiting far too long to take what now belongs to us. I climb on the bed. "Spread your legs."

She parts her legs, and I don't waste time before slamming inside her. When she opens wide on a strangled moan, Drake slides between her lips. He grips her head and fucks her mouth while I hold on to her hips and thrust inside her cunt. She gags around his dick while I slam into her. "Fuck, you feel so good."

She doesn't take part. I know she will say she didn't want this, but she has no choice. She will come for us. Reaching underneath her, I pinch her clit, causing her to whimper as Drake groans, "Fuck Sunshine, your tears are beautiful."

Natalia cries, and Drake plugs her nose as she gasps for breath. I rub her clit while I continue fucking her and then he lets go so she can breathe through her nose again, and she comes violently, her cunt clenches my cock, as her back arches, and she screams as much as she can with a dick in her mouth. My brother finishes in her mouth while I finish in her sweet pussy.

Drake pulls out of her mouth with a glare, "Fucking swallow or I will get dressed and go kill her. Letting her go means nothing. Do as you're told or she's dead."

I can't see her face, but I assume she swallowed when he says, "That's our girl."

Natalia gets up and folds her arms over her chest. Her eyes dart between the two of us with pure anger. "Can I at least sleep in a different room?"

Drake chuckles as he steps toward her and takes her chin into his hands. Tilting her head back, he smirks, "No, Sunshine, you may not. You'll sleep between us, and you won't get out of bed without permission."

I fight the laughter because I know he wants to make sure my cock doesn't come near him. I would never touch my brother sexually, but if a part of our bodies touch, it's not the end of the world.

Natalia glares at Drake. "I wonder what Domenic is going to think about this."

Before he makes a move, I know it's coming. He grabs her by the throat and pushes her down onto the bed as she struggles in his grip. Drake squeezes slightly, restricting her breathing but not completely cutting it off as I stand watching with a hard cock. Cutting off her air supply is my brother's kink, not mine. Yet, her wiggling helplessly underneath him is my kink. I enjoy seeing her fight him, even though this is not a struggle she'll ever win. Like it or not, we have all the power.

"Spread your fucking legs," my brother growls, while tears stream down Natalia's face. She squeezes her thighs closed tightly, refusing to let him have her. But all three of us know the end result.

He grins sardonically. "Is this the choice you really want to make?"

Loosening his hand on her throat, she coughs out, "Are you going to kill me?"

Drake once again squeezes her throat. "Not before I fuck this sweet little cunt again. Now spread your legs before I kill your sister while you watch, and then I'll finish you off."

Instantly she opens her legs while she trembles underneath him, clearly terrified his words of intent are true, although they aren't. I sincerely doubt Drake even has it in him to end her life, regardless I'd never allow him to take her from us permanently. Her eyes widen as her lips part with a gasp when he plows into her with punishing force. I stand next to her head with my cock in my hand, stroking myself to every little noise she makes.

"Pretend you don't fucking love this, Pretty Little Slut," Drake groans as he rails her like he hates her half as much as she hates him right now. She turns her head to me, watching me as I fuck my fist and I know she likes it even though she'll keep denying it. I run my thumb across her bottom lip. "Suck."

She tightens her lips in refusal. Drake reaches up and plugs her nose, which forces her to open her mouth, and I insert two fingers. "Suck." Listening to her gag when I hit the back of her throat with my fingers takes me over the edge. Ropes of my cum land on her cheeks, lips, and neck. I'm not so much of an asshole, so I intentionally avoid her eyes. Her body arches, lips part as she cries out. I remove my fingers while I watch her cum soaked face as she writhes in pleasure. Drake groans as he finishes inside her pussy while I rub my seed into her skin. When he pulls out, she says matter-of-factly, "I need a shower."

"Our guys packed some of your things. Everything you need should be in the bathroom," Drake says as she gets up to go take a shower. He calls after her, "Don't lock the door."

NATALIA

I stand in the bathroom staring at myself in the mirror. The reflection I can't look away from has the word pig written across her soft abdomen. My sister is with me every moment of every day. As if she's standing behind me with disgust, she shouts out words that permeate my brain.

Slut. Whore. Pig. Not good enough.

I spent years trying to figure out why Nicole hates me so much, but I've never figured it out. And does it really matter? Maybe I didn't do anything to earn her contempt. My lacking could be all it took. Knowing the true reason won't change the fact that she can't stand me.

After grabbing my cosmetic bag, I zip it open and glance inside, in an instant relief floods me.

It's here.

I turn on the enormous shower. It has a large shower head on all three black granite walls. It takes me a minute to realize there's a control on the wall so you can use one, two or all three waterfalls. Grabbing my razor blade from my bag, I step into the shower and under the warm water.

Taking the blade, I cut the inside of my upper arm, hissing at the sting. This is my preferred spot because as long as my arms are not raised, it's not noticeable. I hold my arm away from the water as the pain clears my mind; the blood streaming down to my fingertips. I close my eyes and enjoy the silence. When I cut, the ridicule that plays constantly in my mind fades away. The dislike from my mother and my sister. The pure hatred aimed at me by my father. It all lays dormant.

My peace is short-lived as the shower door is yanked open by a furious Drake. "What the fuck are you doing?"

I stand staring blankly at him because I don't know how to respond or if I even need to. I have a razor blade in my left hand. Blood drips from my right one and I think it's obvious what I'm doing. He doesn't give a shit about me. Nobody does. So I don't understand why he appears to be so angry. Although pissed off seems to be his default setting. Dante rushes into the bathroom with concern etched on his face. My gaze darts between the two of them as Drake holds his hand out. "Give me the fucking blade."

I still stand frozen on the spot as I attempt to figure out what to do. I can't let him have it, that much I know. Because I need it. Someone who doesn't cut will never understand. If you don't need the physical pain to numb the emotional, you can't comprehend it.

"Now Natalia," Drake orders.

Chapter Seventeen

DRAKE

She stands holding that fucking razor blade for dear life like it's some kind of a goddamn life line. My immediate concern is her safety. Natalia is gripping the blade so tight, it's cutting her hand. Blood drips from her arm on one side, and from her hand on the other. I rush into the shower, grab her arm that has the blade, twisting it behind her back as I spin her and slam her into the wall.

"Fucking drop it, Natalia. I swear to fucking God if you don't, I'll break your arm."

Do I want to hurt her that badly? No, I really fucking don't, but she'll live with a broken arm. If she cuts too deep or the wrong spot, our girl might end up dead. And I can't allow that to happen. The sobs that come from her are loud and desperate as the bloody blade falls to the shower floor. Dante comes into the shower on her other side. Turning her around to face me, her face is drenched with tears, I think, since the showerhead was only hitting her side. Once I let go of her arm, she slides to the ground with a thump. Both my brother and I lower ourselves to the floor with her.

I wrap my arms around her, pulling her tight against my chest. He strokes her hair while whispering to her, "It's okay." I have no idea what the fuck is happening right now.

"Is this about us fucking you?"

Natalia tilts her head back and gazes at me as she shakes her head. "No."

This is what I wanted, right? Her crying, broken in front of me. I wanted to be the one to break her. I wanted it, but not like this. The thought that someone other than me hurt her makes me see red.

"Who did this to you? Who made you cry?" I ask as she shivers in my arms.

She's ours, and no one may hurt her. Any man that does will die. It's simple. I may spank her, cut off her air supply and make her scream and cry, but no one else gets to do this to Natalia.

"My sister," she whispers against my skin, "She calls me fat and worthless. I guess I believed her."

Dante kisses the back of her head, "You're not fat. You definitely aren't worthless. Natalia, you're fucking perfection."

My brother wants to make everything better for her, take away all the pain. I want information. I want to understand why she cuts her beautiful skin. And I want to kill her fucking trash sister.

"This is why you want to cut your flesh?"

Pulling back from me, her eyelashes flutter lightly as she lifts her gaze to mine. "It's not a want, it's a need. I need to cut. It dulls her voice. I can't explain it, but it lessens the pain."

I take her face in my hands. "If you need pain, I'll give it to you without risking your life. There's an artery in that beautiful arm of yours. You won't do this again. Give us your pain, every fucking ounce of it. If you still need to cut someone, you'll cut me."

Dante grabs her hair and yanks her head back. Pressing his mouth to her neck, he growls, "There's no way that you believe her, Sunshine. No fucking way a woman as beautiful as you could ever buy into those vile words."

She whimpers from the sting from him pulling her hair. "You can convince anyone of anything if you tell them the same things repeatedly."

Natalia isn't wrong. I witnessed it with my brother Domenic's wife, Giada. Abuse is damaging and lasting. The ramifications of it don't disappear when the abuse stops. Did it stop? Or is this ongoing?

I glance at Dante, and he nods as if I said anything. I didn't, but that's the connection we have. Silent conversations became our expertise years ago. He gets out of the shower as I shut the water off. After I help her stand, he wraps a fluffy warm towel around her body and lifts her into his arms and carries her into the bedroom.

Once my brother and Natalia are in bed, I climb in on the other side of her. She lies on her back, her eyes wide open but glazed over like she's not here. She's somewhere else deep inside her mind. Dante kisses her neck, but she doesn't respond at all. I need to find out more about what her sister has done to her. It's obvious that it's a different family dynamic than the one I have with mine. I know she doesn't want us to hurt her sister. The only reason she's here with us right now is to protect her. Yet, I cannot comprehend why. Her sister has been cruel enough to her that she cuts herself. Why the fuck would you protect someone like that? Anybody other than Natalia would've simply told us to kill her. It confuses me and intrigues me at the same time.

After she falls asleep, I motion to Dante silently that I want to talk to him. We both get out of bed, leaving her sleeping peacefully, and grab sweatpants and pull them on. I glance back at Natalia quickly. She lies on her back; her lashes flutter slightly as she breathes softly through parted lips. She is so fucking stunning. I shake my head at myself as I walk to the kitchen with my brother behind me. Natalia is fucking with my head. I want to punish her, yet I want to protect her. There's a strong urge for me to destroy anyone who has ever hurt her, starting with her fucking sister. I shouldn't care. I just wanted to fuck her. But I do care, far more than I'm willing to admit.

Dante stands staring at me when I call Benji telling him I want fucking everything on the Grant family. Every single piece of information on the sister and her parents. No stone is to be left unturned. I need to know every way she's been hurt. Once I have that information, people will pay.

"She's going to be really pissed if you kill Nicole."

I shrug nonchalantly, like it doesn't matter because it doesn't.

"She'll get over it. If her own fucking sister hurt her enough to make her cut herself, she needs to die. We both know there isn't another option. Anyone that causes harm to what's ours is dealt with in the same way. Her family will be no different."

Dante grabs two glasses from the cabinet and pours us both two fingers of whiskey. He hands me one before leaning against the counter. "Agreed, but you better be prepared for one pissed off woman. She might actually cut you."

I grin while I imagine our sweet woman losing it on me. That's exactly what I want from her. Natalia exploding and fighting for herself is exactly what I'm hoping for. I know enough about her family already to know she takes whatever she's given. She doesn't stand up for herself, and that pisses me off.

"I fucking hope she does."

Dante chuckles lightly, "She's right, you are a psycho."

I don't inform my brother that it's not about wanting her to cause me pain, but about her standing up to fight for herself instead of bottling everything inside. I don't particularly enjoy pain, but I am not afraid of it either. When I told her I'd rather she hurt me than herself, I was being sincere. She's different from the women I normally fuck. My normal type is beautiful like she is, but not damaged and not good. *She's so fucking good.* Natalia is good to everyone except herself, and it drives me fucking crazy.

He sets his empty glass on the counter. "So what's the plan?"

"We'll start with the sister. If we don't get what we need, we'll move on to the parents."

While I'm not planning to kill her parents, things could change depending on what I find out. If we determine they have hurt her, then they will also die. The information we've gathered on Natalia isn't enough. There are more holes than a slice of swiss cheese. If she won't be forthcoming with the information, I will find it through other means.

Chapter Eighteen

NATALIA

Sleeping between two dangerous men shouldn't have been possible. Fear alone should've kept me awake all night long, yet I slept like a baby. Opening my eyes, the first thing I see is Drake, pressed against me, but I feel Dante against my back. I try to get away from both of them, but Drake tightens his hold around my shoulders, pulling me against his chest, while Dante's fingers dig into my hip.

"Pretty girl, you aren't going anywhere," Drake says against my neck. His voice is dark and husky, but it's his breath on my skin that causes shivers to roll down my spine. Drake's lips graze my neck while his brother's tongue travels down my back. Drake turns to his back and pulls me on top of him. "Straddle my hips. I need to get inside that pretty pussy."

I move into the position he wants me in, feeling slightly sore from last night, and he grabs my hips and slams into me, causing me to yelp from the intrusion. I jump slightly when Dante rubs circles around my asshole. He chuckles lightly, "Has anybody fucked this beautiful ass, baby?"

"No," I nearly yell with urgency, "I don't want-"

Drake smacks my ass. "We take what we want, Natalia. If my brother wants that beautiful asshole, he'll take it. Understood?"

A tear trickles down my cheek as I glare at him before nodding, "Yes. I fucking get it."

He wraps his arms around my back and pulls me onto his chest, gripping me firmly so I can't move as Dante spreads my ass cheeks, causing me to whimper with fear.. Drake spreads his legs and speaks to his brother, "If your balls fucking touch me, I'm cutting your dick off."

My giggles are short-lived when Dante pushes another finger inside me. I cry out. Drake holds me down firmer in a near crushing grip. Every muscle in my body tenses when I feel the head of his cock pushing inside my ass.

"Relax, Sunshine. Stop fighting."

Drake moves one of his hands to my face. Leaning down, he captures my lips in a slow, tantalizing kiss, causing me to moan, and Dante pushes further into my ass. The pain is nearly blinding as they both move.

"How does that feel?" Drake asks.

"Full. I feel full."

He chuckles as he slams his hips up, hitting a spot deep inside me that threatens to make me come undone.

"Two dicks inside you. Our beautiful little slut likes it this way," Drake groans.

I dig my fingers into Drake's chest as Dante picks up speed, his hands holding my ass firmly as he slams into my ass with punishing force. They both fuck me like men possessed and as much as I know I shouldn't like it, a powerful orgasm hits me, and causes a chain reaction in both brothers.

Drake groans as he fills my pussy, followed by Dante in my ass. I'm going to be oozing cum for days, thanks to both men. We haven't had a single conversation about birth control. It's probably a talk we need to have, but I have bigger priorities at the moment.

"I have to pee."

They both chuckle, and Drake lets me up. "Bathroom and then shower."

Getting up on shaky legs, I make my way to the expensive bathroom and go to the bathroom and wash my hands. As I turn the shower on, both men follow in behind me. I arch an eyebrow at both of them. "I can't shower alone?"

Drake grins sardonically. "No, baby. We want every single second with you until we have to leave for work."

I step into the shower, and both brothers get in, one on each side of me. "Am I allowed to leave?"

Dante chuckles loudly, the sound reverberating through his chest, "Of course. You aren't a prisoner, Sunshine."

Am I not? I disagree. Unless, maybe, they're done with me? Why does that thought make my chest hurt?

"So I'll go home then, after we're done here."

Drake instantly grips my hair and pulls me into his chest. "You aren't a prisoner, but you are ours. Go do whatever you want, but you come back here. If you aren't here by six o'clock in the evening, we'll consider you in breach of contract. And I think you know what happens next."

My sister dies.

He lets me go and Dante gets shampoo and starts washing my hair. I close my eyes and imagine none of this is happening. Sex with both brothers was over the top incredible, but it still isn't what I want. I don't want to be trapped by two mafia men. And hell, how about a little consent?

"I'm going to see Nicole today," I tell them both as Drake washes my body. His hands freeze momentarily on my now soapy breasts. "That's fine. Just know we are watching you. Don't do anything stupid."

I glance up at Drake's stern expression and shrug. "Also, I can't be here at six. I have a show at seven tonight."

He gazes at me with surprise. "Since when?"

I giggle with delight at his, clearly not knowing about my change in plans. Drake thinks he knows everything, but obviously he didn't know about this.

"Last minute."

Drake pinches both of my nipples, causing me to yelp and him to chuckle. "Just behave yourself. Fuck around and find out, Sunshine."

I gaze at him in confusion. "Why do you call me that?"

He doesn't answer, instead Dante does as he comes up behind me, running his nose along my neck, "You're like seeing the sun for the first time after being locked in solitary confinement for a lifetime. You are bright, warm and everything we don't deserve. Yet, we're evil men, so we'll take you, anyway."

I don't know what to say to that, so I say nothing. They'll grow tired of me and move on. Then I'll be free to go back to my life as pathetic as it is. Maybe Nicole will see the sacrifice I've made for her and we can fix things between us. Maybe I'm slightly delusional, but what the hell do I have if I don't have hope?

Drake wraps his hand around my throat, causing me to move back until I crash into Dante's chest.

"You're fucking beautiful, Pretty Girl but don't get confused. That tight pussy won't save anyone if you don't do as you're told. We not only expect complete submission, we fucking demand it. Be a good girl and nobody gets hurt."

This entire situation is beyond confusing. I should be angry with them both. There's no way I should be turned on with his hands around me like this, threatening me. Yet I cannot control the throbbing in my core.

"You don't own me," I say through several gasps. Drake tightens his grip while Dante's cock presses against my back.

Drake smirks slightly. "I own every part of you, Sunshine. That tight little pussy. Those perfect lips. All those sexy moans. And your breath. They are all mine. *Ours*."

He releases his hand from my burning throat, and I cough while trying to control my raspy breathing.

"My heart is mine. It will never be yours."

I turn and race out of the shower to get the hell out of here when I hear Drake chuckle, "You can have that. I don't fucking want it."

Asshole. Of course, it doesn't matter whether he wants my heart. I'd never give it to either of them. They can force me to have sex with them, but they can't make me have feelings I don't and never will. So why did it bother me when he said those words to me? I don't know. There's only one thing I'm certain of. I'm going to buy another razor blade today. Guaranteed after I see Nicole, I'll need it. Drake and Dante may think they control my actions, but they don't. I learned a long time ago to take care of myself. Trust me, if you don't give yourself what you need, no one else will. There's only one person I can count on in this world. *Myself.*

Chapter Nineteen

NATALIA

Sitting in my sister's favorite cafe on nineteenth street, she stares at me with disgust as I take a bite of my blueberry muffin. Instantly, I push it away when I notice her arched eyebrow. She sits drinking a black coffee, not because she likes it that way but because she doesn't consume sugar. None. When we were twelve, she eliminated sugar from her diet. I've never understood how she did it. Everything seems to have some kind of sweetener in it. Nicole, mostly, eats chicken and vegetables for dinner and one egg for breakfast. I've never wondered why she's so much thinner than I am. It's always been clear as day.

"You are what you eat, Natalia. If you eat like a pig, you look like one."

"This pig saved your life. Are you aware of that?"

She takes a sip of her bitter coffee and sets it on the table, eyeing me suspiciously as if she has no clue what I'm talking about. "What?"

Rolling my eyes at her, I say, "Did you think the brothers let you go for no reason? You stole from them. What were you thinking?"

Nicole doesn't respond. She simply stares into her coffee like it's going to answer all her life's problems. Of course, it won't.

"When did you begin using drugs?"

She shrugs like it's not a big deal when it very much is. Clearly, my sister has never been a good person, but a drug addict? It completely blindsided me. I'm not sure if she's addicted to anything, but she must be, right? Unless you were completely addicted and in desperate need, I can't fathom risking your life by stealing from the De Luca brothers. I personally wouldn't take that decision lightly.

"After you were attacked. Remember the pills they gave you that you were too good to take?"

I sigh heavily because I wasn't too good at taking them. In fact, I took two of them but stopped because I didn't like the way they made me feel. Groggy, lightheaded, and completely out of it. I noticed the bottle had disappeared from the nightstand, but I said nothing because I assumed my mom probably disposed of them after realizing I wasn't taking them. Obviously, I was wrong.

"You've been taking pills for that long?"

She shakes her head, "No. You don't just stay on painkillers. It escalates."

Her words confuse me even more than I already was. If she didn't steal pills from them, then what was it?

"What did you steal from them?"

Nicole sits across from me in blue jeans and a white blouse, looking like a model, not a junkie. This isn't what I picture a drug user looking like. Her blonde hair hangs past her shoulders, straightened perfectly, her makeup flawless as always. That's how I've always seen her. *Flawless. Perfect. Everything I'll never be.*

"Meth and heroin," she answers, as I instantly gasp. She continues, "I didn't steal from the brothers. It was some low-level dealer."

I shake my head in disgust as I sip my sweet coffee. "He couldn't have been that low level if he works for the De Luca family."

She doesn't argue for once. "Yeah, well, I didn't know that. Obviously. Anyway, how exactly did you save my life?"

When I tell her how I've had to give myself to the two brothers until they are done using me like I'm a literal sex doll, her expression is filled with disbelief.

"That can't be. It makes no sense whatsoever. They could've had me," she says as she flips her hair behind her shoulder like she's as perfect as I almost believe her to be. Then she laughs like someone told the funniest joke she's ever heard.

"Seriously. What do they *really* want?"

I'm not sure if it pisses me off more that she got me into this mess or the fact that she thinks it's preposterous that any man could ever find me attractive, let alone two. As much as it annoys me, I agree with her even though I won't admit it to her. The biggest reason is because my experience has always been that men are into me until they see my sister. So them having the choice to have her, but choosing me instead is different.

Okay, they didn't really choose me.

It's not as if they are in love with me, I know that. Still, they fucked me instead of Nicole. That's a first and I'll take it even though I don't understand it.

"So you fucked them *both?*"

I nod with a giggle, "Yeah, I did."

My sister, who will fuck anything that moves, looks at me with disapproval, "Pig and slut," she says under her breath, knowing full well I can hear her.

Her dark gaze stares at me suspiciously. "What do they want, though? I don't get it."

I shrug because I don't know why, either. "Me, I guess."

Nicole leans forward as if she's going to tell me a secret. "No. That can't be it. There's something you're missing. That can't possibly be the reason."

Any normal person would say my sister is a bitch and disregard everything she says to me. That would be the logical reaction. I've always been far more emotional than logical. So her words hit me in the heart. She's right, there has to be a reason. They had Nicole after they took her. Guaranteed, she would've fucked them because this is Nicole, after all. I know they didn't do anything with her because had they, my sister would be happy to throw it in my face. The bigger question is, why do I care? Drake made it clear that they'd fuck me until they were done. When will they be done? And will I survive it?

DRAKE

We mostly trust Natalia to do as she's told, but that didn't stop us from having eyes on her when she met with her sister for breakfast. My guy has followed her all day long. She took one bite of a muffin and then pushed it away. She ate nothing for lunch. I won't ignore the fact that she's not taking care of herself. She'll be punished. And fed. After I feed her my cock, she'll eat food for nourishment.

After meeting with her sister, she went to a pharmacy and purchased several items. I don't have a problem with most of her shopping spree. All of them were fine except for one.

Razor blades. Sneaky little girl.

That will bring an even harsher punishment than not eating. The punishment I will administer isn't one of shaming her or making her feel worse than she already does. The pain I'll deliver is exactly what Natalia needs. My pretty little pain slut.

I pull up to the club where she's performing tonight. Dante was called to help Damian and Domenic with a shipment issue, so I'm on my own with our girl. Not exactly a hardship. I walk into *Bellissima*, the club Domenic bought a little over a year ago. People might think that's how Natalia got this job, because of her connection to my brother's wife, but it's not. Our sweet girl is talented in her own right. She doesn't need the De Luca family to pull any strings for her. While I know enough about her, I'm aware playing the piano and singing was not her dream. She's made the best of it. She'd prefer to be dancing across a stage with a ballet company. Her injury broke her heart. Natalia is resilient. She may have been knocked down, but she picked herself back up. She's stronger than she knows. By the time we're done with her, she will be a fierce woman who knows her worth. We'll leave our girl better than we found her.

Walking into the club, I nod at the doormen. Normally, there's a cover charge however, as a De Luca brother, of course, I won't pay one. I walk through the set of double leather doors and make my way to my table. Most of the club is decorated in dark blue. To my right is a black bar with matching tall leather chairs. There are about two hundred round black tables. Each one has a hurricane candle as the lone decoration. Domenic wanted to keep things simple and elegant. My favorite part of this entire establishment is the shiny black grand piano where my girl will sit and play for the packed club. I glance at my watch as I take my seat at my small table and see that she'll be out in approximately two minutes. Under normal circumstances, I have incredible patience. Nothing rattles me. Yet waiting for her does. I haven't seen her since she left this morning. I've had eyes on her, but it's not the same. My nerves of steel are long gone by the time she makes her way to the piano. Like the planets have finally aligned, I can breathe a sigh of relief when I have her in my sights.

Chapter Twenty

NATALIA

There's that part in romance movies when the female character can't see the male character, yet she knows he's there. Their connection is so strong she can feel him. That's how I feel right now. I know Drake is here. His presence is larger than life and he exudes power. Maybe it's not that we have a connection, but it's just his way. Maybe everybody can feel him this way. However, when I take a seat at the piano, I turn my head and immediately I'm locked in his gaze. My eyes travel from his stern expression down to his white button-down shirt, the first few buttons undone, exposing his colorful skull tattoo at the base of his neck. He smirks at me as my gaze moves back up to his face. I watch as an attractive blonde waitress with a perfect body approaches him. He speaks to her, but his attention stays on me completely. It's as if he sees no one other than me. I won't let it go to my head though, because this is probably one big power trip. That's why he wants me, only because he can control everything. I force myself to focus on the piano as my fingers strike the keys.

I think the reason I've been successful in this career is because most pianists that play in clubs simply perform well-known songs. However, I wrote my music mostly, with the occasional cover thrown in. While people enjoy hearing songs, they know the crowd has become familiar, so a lot of my songs are no longer new to them. Some of my songs are instrumental, but more than a few have vocals as well. The people who come to see me seem to enjoy it. I don't call them fans even when I know they come for me. That seems uppity and pretentious, two things I never aspire to be. Closing my eyes, I sing about love and loss while the crowd sits quietly, as if they are focusing on every single word that flows from my mouth. When I look out at the people, most of them have eyes on me, but not like Drake. He stares at me with an intensity that nearly melts me to the core. His gaze makes me feel exposed in a room full of people, as if they can see every part of me, even the parts I desperately want to hide. I take a deep breath and focus on the keys. Every note, every chord, the emotions, the words that come from my broken soul.

Cuts so deep.

Watch me bleed.

Feel the pain.

See me die.

A little each day.

Broken in pieces.

Nothing left to mend.

You took the only thing I need.

Me.

I have nothing left to give.

You win.

When I look back at Drake as I finish the last few notes of the song, I notice something I didn't think he was capable of. He appears to be overcome with emotion. Is it possible the big evil monster has a heart, after all?

I stand beside the piano, giving the audience my thanks as they clap and cheer. While I know Drake is watching me like a toddler that might take off running at any moment, I decide to act like I normally would. Walking over to him, I announce, "I'm getting a drink."

His glare game is strong as he arches an eyebrow in disapproval, "One drink, Sunshine. Then we're going home."

Crossing my arms over my chest, I roll my eyes. "I don't have a home. Remember? Some psycho burned it to the ground."

The muscles in his jaw clench as his eyes darken to near blackness, "Natalia," he growls, the sound reverberating through his chest, "One drink. Don't test me, pretty girl."

I don't respond. I flip my hair over my shoulder, giving him all of my attitude, and walk over to the bar.

DRAKE

This beautiful woman is pushing all my goddamn buttons. I'm ready to snap and carry her out of her caveman style. Natalia is

119

fucking clueless about all the men staring at her like they have a fucking chance in hell with my girl. She smiles and talks amongst her fans, takes her drink and sips it before thanking the bartender. I don't think she even noticed when I stood up and followed her while her sassy ass went to the bar. My blood boils as I spot a man grabbing her arm and she simply allows it. Finally, she attempts to pull her arm free, but he wraps his other hand around her waist and pulls her into his chest. Wrong move on the wrong fucking girl, dickhead.

He lowers his head like he's going to kiss her when I get close enough for him to hear me. "Put your slimy tongue anywhere near my woman and I'll cut it out."

His gaze snaps from her to me. "Your woman?"

I nod, "Yeah. She's mine. So kindly remove your fucking hands from my woman before I remove them for you."

His gaze moves up and down my body as if he's sizing me up but makes a life saving decision and lets her go.

"Natalia. Let's go."

I expect her to argue, but she doesn't, which is good because I'd carry her out over my shoulder if it was necessary. Taking her hand in mine, I extend her arm so I can make sure she's okay, but instantly see red indentations from the asshole's fingers.

"Does it hurt?"

She nods. "A little, but I'll be okay. I've had worse."

Leaning down, I kiss her marks gently before motioning for Jack, one bouncer, to come over to us. When he does, I give him instructions. "Stay with her. I'm going to take care of the dick that assaulted her."

While it's technically his job to handle this situation, he knows better than to argue with me about it. Walking over to the man who touched what's mine, I pull my fist back, and it lands square on his jaw. He stumbles all over the place while grabbing his face, moaning in pain, and I pull my arm back and hit again in the same spot.

"Keep your hands off my woman. Next time you die."

Immediately, I turn back to a horrified Natalia and tell Jack, "Escort him outside. He is not to be permitted entrance again."

I take her uninjured hand in mine and walk her outside to my waiting driver. Once I help her inside, I instruct the driver, "La Fontaine."

After raising the privacy glass, I take her hand and look at her arm again. I don't like the way my chest tightens when I see red marks on her flawless skin. Which is irony at its finest, considering she looks beautiful when I mark her. Natalia closes her eyes and moans lightly as I run my fingers over the spot where he squeezed. That little black dress with the low cut 'V' is begging to be ripped from her delicious body. Wrapping my hand around her throat, her eyes snap open, and pure lust fills her gaze, "Dirty fucking girl. You love it when I steal your breath, don't you?"

She doesn't speak as I squeeze slightly, but she nods in agreement. I place my hand around her waist and dash her to the other side. Lying her down on the seat, I climb over her, pressing my lips to hers and take what I've wanted since she walked out onto that stage.

Her mouth opens on a moan and I push my tongue against hers. Natalia reaches up and runs her fingers through my hair, causing me to groan. She digs her nails into my scalp and it makes me go feral. The car slows to a stop, but I'm desperate to watch her come. I hold myself up and tell her, "Spread your legs."

Wasting no time, I reach between her thighs and reach my hand inside her panties and thrust two fingers inside her wet pussy. Tossing her head back, she cries out when my thumb brushes against her clit. Every time I pull my fingers out, she thrusts her hips up, chasing the friction she needs.

"Greedy pretty girl, come for me."

Her eyes glaze over as she tightens around my fingers and cries my name. Fuck. My name falling from her lips does something to me. My cock is hard as a rock and I want nothing more than to slam inside her, but I won't. I will torture myself because my girl needs to eat. I pull my fingers out of her cunt and push them into my mouth so I can taste her. She watches me with renewed desire, "Want a taste, pretty girl?"

Leaning forward, I kiss her, making her taste herself on my tongue. Some women aren't into this, but mine is. She sucks on my tongue, taking her flavor from me, and within seconds, my dick is ready to burst into my pants.

"Come on, baby."

She lays there appearing sated with a smirk on her face, "What if I'm not hungry?"

I raise an eyebrow in annoyance. "You will eat. Or there will be severe consequences. Besides, you're going to need the sustenance to get through tonight."

While I have no problem sharing my little toy with my brother, I'm happy to get to spend time alone with her.

"Why is that?" She asks innocently, as if she doesn't know.

Rubbing my thumb over her bottom lip, I groan when she bites the digit.

I chuckle lightly. "I'm going to fuck until you can no longer stay awake. Then when you finally fall asleep, I'm going to fuck you again. Now let's go."

Helping her up, I open the door and get out and help her to the street.

La Fontaine is a restaurant my brother Damian owns. Under normal circumstances, I might be concerned about him dropping in and seeing us together, but I know he's busy with Domenic and Dante tonight.

Her eyes sparkle as she smiles widely. "This is Kat's favorite restaurant. I've heard so much about it."

This entire thing started because I simply wanted to fuck her. Natalia's happiness was never part of the equation. Yet seeing her smile like this makes me wonder if I could have the impossible. Then I remember her words, *"You'll never have my heart."*

She would be right to keep that from me. Long-term commitments are not my thing. I'll never be able to give her what she needs. Maybe my brother can, but I can't. I will need to let her go, but not yet. For tonight, she's mine, only mine.

Chapter Twenty—One

NATALIA

This meal with Drake is anxiety inducing. I have food issues, and the thought of eating like a pig in front of him is devastating. I know he doesn't love me and never will, but the way he looks at me like he's constantly dying to fuck me is addicting. *Relax Natalia.* I'll get a chicken salad or something light like that. No carbs. Whoever created carbohydrates should be killed. They were probably created by Satan himself. The more you eat, the more you crave.

We walk through the restaurant and go into a private dining room. He pulls out a chair for me, and I take a seat before he pushes my chair in. I hide my surprise at his chivalrous behavior. It's unexpected but pleasant just the same.

He takes a seat across from me and I ask, "I assume someone will bring a menu?"

Shaking his head, he says, "No. I'll be ordering for you. I don't need a menu because I have it memorized."

"I just want a salad."

He chuckles, "You aren't a fucking rabbit, pretty girl. There's one rule tonight, only one. Do as you're fucking told."

Lowering my gaze to the table, I practically beg, "Drake, please."

The waitress appears and I realize quickly he won't relent as he orders.

"Two glasses of red wine, you know my preference. Grilled medium steaks for two, along with mashed potatoes, seasonal vegetables and a selection of bread, please."

He arches an eyebrow in my direction. "And a side salad for my little bunny."

Drake seems to have the impression that I like salad, which I guess it's okay, but that's not why I wanted one.

The waitress walks away and he instantly questions me as he sits back in his chair, "You aren't happy with what I ordered for you?"

I shrug like it doesn't matter, but to me, it does. "It's fine, just so many carbs."

He places his hand over mine. "You don't like them?"

I laugh a little louder than I mean to, "Drake, I've never met a carb I didn't like. That's the problem honestly. I'm trying to be less of a pig."

My words seem to anger him as he slams a fist on the table. "Natalia," he growls sexily, "Do you want to see me angry, pretty girl?"

"Not especially," I answer as the waitress comes back and places our wine glasses on the table in front of us. "Anything else, Sir?"

I roll my eyes at the way she stares at him with hope, like he might tell her to drop to her knees and suck his cock. Luckily for me, he doesn't. I mean nothing to him, so I'm not sure why it matters, but it does. The way he gives her no attention makes my heart swell with some sort of misplaced pride. Drake's gaze stays firmly affixed to mine as he responds to the annoying blonde, "No. That'll be all."

He takes a sip of his wine while I do the same. Then he asks for the one thing I don't know that I can give him.

"Tell me where this pig thing comes from."

I shake my head, refusing to talk about this with him. Drake isn't some soft-hearted, supportive guy. My worst fear is that if I tell him about this, he'll laugh. I don't think I could bear hearing him enjoying my horror.

He arches an eyebrow in obvious annoyance. "Do you think you're safe because we are in public, pretty girl? I assure you, I don't care where we are. I will spank that beautiful ass until you give me exactly what I want."

Folding my arms over my chest, I return his glare. "You wouldn't dare."

His chuckle causes goosebumps to move across my skin. He wouldn't do that here, would he? We are in his brother's restaurant. Surely this brute has limits. Without a word, he rises from his seat and begins moving our wine glasses and silverware to the side of the table while I observe him with a confused expression.

"Stand," he says, but I know it's not a request, it's an order, so I do.

He grips the back of my neck and pushes me over the now empty table. I turn my head to the side so I can breathe, "Drake, please."

His laughter sounds out before me. "Are you ready to talk, pretty girl?"

"No," I answer honestly. If he thinks this will make me want to confide in him, he's very wrong. Humiliating me in a restaurant is not the answer he thinks it is. Drake grabs the hem of my dress on either side and yanks it over my hips and then hooks his thumbs into the sides of my panties and pulls them down my legs until they are pooled at my feet. I whimper when he slides his hands up my thighs to my bare ass and squeezes my flesh. "I know, pretty girl. The sooner you learn how to do as you're told, the easier this will be."

Squeezing my eyes shut, I blurt out, "I fucking hate you."

He chuckles like it's the greatest thing he's ever heard. "Good."

Before I can question his response, his hand comes down on my flesh, *hard.* He quickly strikes me again. I moan loudly because the pain is intense and exactly what I need. The stinging pain is a relief. It's as if with every hit he quiets her voice. The demon in my mind that constantly reminds me that I'm not good enough.

Don't eat so much. Lose weight. Be who they want you to be.

He hits me again, with so much force, my body moves forward as I cry out. Drake groans when he runs his finger along my wet slit.

"Fuck. You're drenched for me, pretty girl."

The clanging of his belt buckle is loud in the room, with nothing other than soft music playing. I should tell him no, but would he stop if I did? It doesn't matter because if I'm honest with myself; I want

128

this as much as he does. Drake groans as he pushes into me with urgency. He makes me feel like he'll die without me and I'm well aware what a dangerous thought process this is with this man. Again, I remind myself to not get attached to him. This is temporary, after all. When the brothers both get their fill, I'll be tossed aside like trash. He pulls out most of the way and slams back into me repeatedly. Drake wraps his hand around the side of my neck so I can't move. I whimper underneath his powerful frame, "Someone could come in."

My concern is met with him chuckling, the deep sound vibrating against my back as he speaks directly into my ear, "Then you better hurry and come for me, pretty girl. I can go all night long."

"I can't," I whimper louder than I intend to.

He pulls me up slightly, wraps his hand around my throat while he continues fucking me. "You'll breathe again when you do as you're told."

I squirm in his grip, but he only tightens his hold on me. I panic as he cuts my breath off completely. The black spots in my vision cause the fear to grow as my body gives in to him. He eases up on my throat as the orgasm crashes in on me. I gulp for air, causing me to cough repeatedly.

Drake pounds into me, chasing his own release, and groans, "You're so fucking beautiful when you're obedient for me."

The door opens and a man with our food walks in and Drake barks at him, "Out. Now."

He quickly averts his gaze, places our food on the table and quickly races out.

"I should fucking kill him for seeing you like this."

Drake pulls out of me and yanks me so I'm standing and grips my chin, "Nobody other than my brother gets to see you like this."

I arch an eyebrow at his absolute absurdity. "It's your fault. If it weren't for you, I wouldn't have been bent over a table being fucked."

His lips turn up into a devious grin as he says, "Get on your knees, pretty girl. Clean up the mess you've made."

Drake pulls my panties back up and fixes my skirt. "Do as you're told."

"You have control issues."

Grabbing me by the shoulders, he pushes me down to my knees. I lift his cock and lick the underside, causing him to groan, before taking him into my mouth and sucking him clean. I taste myself on him and wonder, should this disgust me? It doesn't. The flavor of the two of us combined is powerful.

Removing himself from my mouth, he grabs my shoulders and pulls me to my feet as he gazes at me. "That's my good girl. *My beautiful girl.* Now, sit down and eat."

After putting himself back together, he grabs our plates, cutlery, and glasses of wine and puts them back where they were.

DRAKE

I spread butter on a piece of pumpernickel bread and hand it to Natalia. She cringes as if I'm handing her a fucking snake.

"Do I have to?" She asks with profound sadness that I simply don't understand. Why should it be so devastating to eat bread?

"Yes. Unless you can give me a valid reason for not at least trying it."

A tear trickles down her cheek and she swipes at it angrily with her free hand, "Please, Drake. Don't make me talk about this."

While I don't enjoy making her cry, I won't let this go because I have a feeling this is why she hurts herself. She stares down at her plate with defeat and shakes her head. "I'm a fat pig. I don't need these carbs."

Her words make me see red in an instant, but I force myself to keep a stoic demeanor and not react. "What makes you say that?"

She wipes another tear away and glances at me momentarily before returning her gaze to her plate of food that she hasn't touched.

"I've been told that my entire life by my sister. I guess when you hear something enough, you believe it."

I cut my steak, hoping she'll follow suit, but she doesn't.

"Is this why you hurt yourself?"

She nods before she speaks quietly, barely above a whisper, "Yes. I don't expect you to understand, but it makes me feel better for a little while. When I cut into my skin, it quiets her voice in my head."

We should've killed her sister when we had her in our warehouse. If I had known what I do now, I would have. Of course, then we wouldn't have had anything to hold over her and she wouldn't be with us now. Still, if I had it to do over again, that bitch would be dead.

"She makes you feel like this and still you saved her life?"

Her wet eyes lift to mine as she stares at me with a shocked expression. "She's my sister. My twin. Of course, I'd save her. It doesn't matter that she hates me. I still love her."

I would lie down my life for any of my brothers without a second thought, but it's not the same. I know if one of them had abused me the way her sister has her, I'd have ended them, sibling or not.

"Two bites of everything. That's the requirement. You are not a fat pig. Natalia, you are fucking stunning. Your sister is a goddamn liar. Maybe she's jealous. I don't know what her issue is, but you are absolute perfection. So be a good girl and eat your dinner, please. I don't want to punish you, but if I have to, I will. You will eat. That's not negotiable."

Chapter Thirty-One

NATALIA

Dinner was pleasant once I told him what he wanted to know, and he didn't laugh at me like I'd expected him to. As soon as we walk into the house, he says, "Give me the razor blades you bought today."

I stand frozen as I swallow hard. "What?"

He crosses his arms over his chest while his glare intensifies, "Do not play games with me, Natalia, give me the fucking razor blades."

"How-"

He cuts me off quickly. "Yes, we will have you watched when you're not with us, pretty girl. It's for your protection."

I raise an eyebrow in annoyance. "Stalking me is for my protection? Was burning my house down also for my benefit?"

Drake shrugs his shoulders with a deep chuckle. "No baby. Burning your house down was most definitely for my benefit."

I open my purse and hand him the razor blades. "I don't understand why you want to hurt me. This is all temporary. And when you both tire of me, I'll have nowhere to go. I will have no choice but to return to my family. The same family that hates me more than you could imagine. I know I mean nothing to you, but why do you want to destroy me? What have I done to you?"

He places the razor blades in the pocket of his black dress pants and races to me. Grabbing my face, he tilts my head back and stares into my eyes with his dark ones. "Pretty girl, I don't know how this ends. I doubt my brother will ever grow tired of you, but I can't speak for him. But me? You're my fucking kryptonite. Even though I know you might destroy me, I can't stay away from you. I'm a powerful man. I always have been, but you make me fucking weak. If you're looking for guarantees on things, I can't give you that. But I promise you, if we let you go, you won't be homeless. We will take care of you even if you aren't ours anymore."

He leans down and swipes my lips with his tongue, causing me to moan his name.

"If you need pain, you tell me and I'll administer it safely. I will not allow you to cut your beautiful skin, to risk your life. I promise you, your sister is not worth it. Now, go upstairs and get changed into the lingerie that's on the bed."

DRAKE

Natalia walks upstairs and I pour myself a drink while I give her time to get changed. After taking a large pull of my whiskey, I set the glass down on the table beside the couch where I sit. Grabbing my phone, I text Dante.

> I want her parents brought to the warehouse.

He doesn't respond, but I'm not surprised because I know it's a busy night. I could be wrong, but I think her parents will tell us everything we need to know. There are things with Natalia that make little sense. Maybe none of it should matter as long as we get what we want from our pretty girl, but for some reason, it does. I want to know everything about her. Then I want to destroy everyone who has ever hurt her, whether they're a blood relation to her or not. I swallow the last gulp of my drink before taking her blades to the garbage outside. When I walk back in, I wash my hands before going upstairs to find my beautiful girl.

Opening the door to the bedroom, my mouth goes dry when I see her. *Jesus.* She stands in the black lacy open bust bustier I bought for her, no panties, matching sheer thigh highs and black heels. Natalia grabs at the bottom lacy hem like she's uncomfortable. I like it when women are sure of themselves, but there's something so sweet and genuine with the way she has no clue how fucking perfect she is.

"Turn around baby."

I can tell by her expression she wants to refuse but thinks better of it and slowly turns. I groan when I see her perfect naked ass. The bustier comes down slightly lower in the front, but her ass is on full delicious display for me.

"Bend over and touch your toes. Show me that beautiful cunt."

135

"Drake," she whimpers desperately.

I walk up behind her, place my hand on her back and nuzzle her forward, "Show me what's mine, pretty girl."

Reluctantly, she does as she's told, and my eyes naturally gravitate to her pussy.

"Fuck. You're exquisite. And mine."

Kneeling behind her, I spread her ass cheeks and press my face to her opening and inhale her scent. Natalia squirms against my hold, but it only makes me grip her tighter. I push my tongue into her pussy and she cries out in what almost sounds like relief. I can't take much more. Tonight, I'll take her the way I've fantasized about for months.

"Lay on the bed. On your back."

I get to my feet as she moves to the bed. Without a word, I climb on the bed beside her and fasten her wrists in the wrist straps. I chuckle at her widened eyes as she stares at me with fear. Kneeling beside her, I brush my thumbs over her exposed, firm nipples. "I will not hurt you, pretty girl. Not tonight anyway."

Getting off the bed, I smirk as she watches me with a hungry gaze as I unbutton my dress shirt. I place the black fabric over the back of the sitting chair before moving to my pants. My eyes stay focused on the beautiful girl in the bed. "Like what you see, needy girl?" I ask as she licks her lips.

"Yes," she speaks so low it's nearly inaudible.

I remove my dress pants and boxers and place them with my shirt. Standing at the foot of the bed, I fist my cock. "Spread your legs. I want to see every inch of that beautiful body."

She does, and I take a moment to let my eyes travel the length of her stunning physique. How this woman even believes anything her vile sister has to say is beyond me. She's exquisite like this. Her arms strapped to the frame of the bed, dressed in black lingerie, her tits falling over the fabric, dark hair hanging down below her shoulders and that pretty exposed pussy beautifully pink and already wet for me.

I climb back onto the bed, grab her legs and push them back, "Tell me you're a beautiful woman."

She shakes her head in defiance. "No. I can't."

I slap her clit hard and she gasps, "Fucking say it. Even if you don't believe it right now, you will say it."

She closes her eyes as if she's in tremendous pain and says words I know she thinks are a lie, "I'm a be-autiful woman," she stumbles as she does what she was told. She said to me before that if you hear something enough, you believe it whether or not it's true. I will tell her she's gorgeous every day and eventually she'll know it to be the truth.

"That's right, pretty girl. You are."

Her eyes pop open and a tear travels down her cheek. I lean down and lick her teardrop, "Tell me what you need, Natalia."

"Pain," she whimpers, "I need pain, Drake. Please. Make it stop."

I close her legs and situate her so her lower half is turned to her side. Climbing off the bed I go over to my dress pants and grab my belt.

"You don't need a safeword, Natalia. If it becomes too much, simply tell me to stop and I will."

With tears falling down her beautiful face, she only says, "Okay."

Kneeling behind her ass on the bed, I hold her one thigh as I strike her ass with the belt, causing her to cry out deliciously. Each time I strike her, she cries out in pain and relief, her skin turning red. I toss the belt onto the floor, knowing she may never tell me to stop, but it's enough. I didn't even want to hurt her, but I did it because this is what she needs. And if it stops her from cutting herself, I'll take a belt to her ass every single day. She winces when I roll her back onto her ass.

"Do I need to untie you so you're not on your ass? I know it must hurt."

Natalia flashes me a stunning smile that causes my chest to squeeze. "No. I like it."

Grabbing a pillow, I place it under her ass to lift her pelvis slightly.

I bend her legs back, holding onto the heels of her shoes as I slide into her cunt, "Pretty little pain slut."

"Drake," she cries out on the first thrust, which only spurs me on. I would do anything to hear her crying out my name repeatedly. It does something to me I can't explain. I want my name falling from her full, pouty lips every day.

Again, she gasps my name as I pound into her. I pull out most of the way, "I know, baby," and slam back into her. She is so fucking gorgeous like this. Natalia may not have wanted this little arrangement in the beginning, release. But she loves this now.

"Hold your left leg back for me."

She does and I wrap my now free hand around her throat, "Come for me, beautiful slut. Squeeze my cock with that ravenous little cunt."

I watch her face as her eyes widen while she struggles for breath. Natalia bucks her hips with every single thrust, giving as good as she takes it. I know she's close, so I ease up on my grip and she inhales, taking in a big gulp of air as an orgasm takes over her gorgeous body. I keep pounding into her as she screams like I've never fucking heard before. Her face is flushed as her eyes roll back into her head while she shudders underneath me.

"Fucking perfect."

I move over top of her, place my left hand beside her on the mattress and cradle her face with my right hand, licking her lips before biting her bottom one, I growl, "You think you're imperfect, Natalia but what I see is a woman that is flawless. This body. Your heart. Every part of you is far more than I deserve. Yet, I'm a selfish bastard, so I'll take it, anyway."

I continue fucking her and she squeaks, "Until you tire of me, right?"

She wraps her legs around my waist as I continue chasing my own release. "Do you think that's even possible, pretty girl? Do you think I could ever live without you? After having you? I sincerely doubt it."

Lifting her head, she kisses me, tangling her tongue with my own as I pump her full of my cum. Yeah, I don't think I can ever let her go. And I know my brother feels the same.

Chapter Thirty-Three

DANTE

It's three in the morning, so I knew when I walked in, both Natalia and Drake would likely be asleep. Walking into the bedroom and finding her wrapped around my brother like he's the only man in the world does something to me I don't like. Until this moment, I thought sharing her wasn't a problem. The way she lays in his arms, her face pressed against his chest, it tells me she didn't miss me. I bet she didn't even think about me for a single second. I'm not used to jealousy. To be honest, I'm not entirely sure how to handle it. If the man in bed with my girl wasn't my brother, he'd already be dead with his blood splattered all over her beautiful body. But he is my brother. And I agreed with this. *Fuck.*

I should go to bed, but I don't. Instead, I strip down to my boxers and take a seat in the oversized chair while I watch my girl snuggle up with Drake. It's pure torture looking at her naked body draped over his. I sit here for hours, sipping on a Scotch, staring at my Natalia. Her eyes peel open and her gaze travels to mine as if she could somehow feel I was here. That's crazy though, right? A lazy smile spreads across her face as she jumps up and rushes over to me, "Dante!" Climbing into my lap, she throws her arms around my neck, "Why didn't you come to bed?"

I shrug slightly as I return her embrace. "I didn't want to interrupt."

Running my fingers down her naked back, I hold her close to me as she arches her back, leaning into my touch. A moan slips from her lips as my cock hardens. I pull myself out of my boxers, lift her and slide her down my length. I glance over her shoulder and see my brother watching us as I grab her ass, lift her and slam her back down onto my cock. Pushing her feet onto the chair on either side of me, she bounces while I take her nipples into my mouth, one and then the other.

"If this is how you'll greet me every time I'm out late, I might be home late more often."

She giggles as she presses her face into my shoulder. "I shouldn't have, but I missed you."

Kissing her neck, I groan louder than I mean to, "I missed you too, sunshine."

The entire night dealing with our missing shipment, I thought about her. It was hell. Knowing my brother was with her and I was stuck dealing with a miserable Domenic. He is the head of our family and has a short temper when things don't go his way. He had no intention of leaving his wife until she gives birth, but this wasn't

142

optional. Drake is lucky he didn't get pulled into it. I didn't mention him helping us because I didn't really want Natalia to be left alone. So this was the lesser of two evils.

"Let me have her mouth," Drake says, but I chuckle because it's not happening.

"I don't think so, asshole. You've had to yourself all night. Now she's mine. I'm not sharing. You can watch or go fuck yourself."

I fist my hand in her hair and pull her mouth to mine and take her in a slow, tantalizing kiss. Lowering my mouth to her neck, I suck on the spot below her ear that makes her pant. She moves up and down my cock, now increasing her speed, almost with desperation.

"Good girl. Make yourself come on my dick, sunshine."

She tosses her head back, her lips part on a loud moan, as her pussy squeezes me like a vice, pulling my orgasm from me.

"Take a shower and come downstairs. I'll make you breakfast."

She arches an eyebrow and feigns a serious expression, "There better be coffee."

I chuckle as I squeeze her against my chest. "Anything for you, sunshine."

Natalia pulls back, places her hands on my face and stares at me in what appears to be confusion. "That's sweet for a mobster, Dante. You aren't supposed to be nice. You're lethal, remember?"

"Only for you, baby. Now go get that shower."

She gets off me, and I put myself back in my boxers before grabbing a pair of sweatpants. I nod to my brother to follow me downstairs so we can discuss his text message from earlier before our girl comes down.

As I'm brewing a pot of coffee, Drake walks into the kitchen. "I assume you got my text."

I nod as I grab three coffee mugs and place them on the counter. "Yeah. I couldn't respond without raising questions with Domenic. It's arranged. Michael will pick all three of them up shortly."

He folds his arms over his chest as he stares at me through a narrowed gaze. "All three of them?"

I pour the cups of coffee. "Yeah. Just in case we need her for leverage."

Handing my brother a cup, he says, "Thanks," as I take a sip of mine.

Natalia comes into the kitchen looking like a fucking dream, dressed in jeans and a skimpy tank top, her pretty little nipples pressing against the thin fabric. "All three of who?"

Drake growls at her, "Business. Our business, not yours."

She rolls her eyes at him, and I chuckle when he doesn't respond to it. That's very unlike my brother, because he has a serious issue with disrespect.

I hand Natalia her coffee, and she inhales the scent before a light moan slips from her. "Thank you. You're a prince."

"That's me," I chuckle before asking, "What do you want to eat?"

She shakes her head and glances at my brother with a nervous expression. "Nothing," Natalia holds her hands up, "I promise I'll eat. I'm having breakfast and spending the day with Giada."

Drake places his coffee cup on the counter and moves to her, cradling Natalia's face in his palms. He speaks low, "If I find out you didn't eat, and I will find out, there will be consequences. Unpleasant consequences."

People bristle under his gaze. Recently, Natalia would've as well, but not this time. She narrows her eyes at him. "I'm not afraid of you, you big brute. But I will eat because I said I would. I'm not a liar. Don't treat me like one."

"Fuck your sexy," he growls, and she giggles, "I'm sexy now?"

He chuckles loudly, "You've always been sexy, pretty girl. You standing up for yourself? Yeah, that's the sexiest thing I've ever seen."

Leaning down, he kisses her. I groan when she moans into his mouth. They separate and she walks over to me and throws her arms around my neck. "Thank you for the coffee."

I rub the pad of my thumb over her bottom lip. "Thank you for riding my cock."

Her cheeks blush instantly as she lowers her gaze in embarrassment. "Dante."

Placing my thumb and finger on her chin and tilt her head back, "No sunshine. You don't get to be ashamed of feeling good."

Standing on her toes, she presses her lips to mine and I kiss her back with more forcefulness than is necessary. Natalia whimpers when

I wrap her hair around my fists and yank her head back so I can devour her slender neck. Fuck. This is what I want her to give herself to me like this. Not because if she doesn't, her pathetic cunt of a sister will die. But because she wants this as much as we do. I groan when she digs her nails into my chest as she melts into me. Drake comes up behind her and she whimpers as she's sandwiched between the two of us.

"Are you wet for us, pretty girl?"

She giggles lightly. "I've been wet since you basically kidnapped me. I have to go. Gia is waiting for me."

My brother grabs her shoulders and spins her until she's facing him. "We did not kidnap you. You have never been treated like a kidnap victim. However, if you'd prefer, I'd be happy to keep you chained to a bed twenty-four seven."

We both chuckle as she visibly shrinks. "No. Please," her voice trembles in a plea to not be locked up like the captive she claims to be.

Drake glares at her, his hands gripping her shoulders. "You want to play the victim, you'll be the victim. Play stupid games, win stupid prizes, pretty girl. Understood?"

She nods emphatically, "Yes."

"Good girl. Now behave yourself today. No stopping at the pharmacy. Got it?"

"Yes," she says bitterly and my brother chuckles, "Who gives you pain when you need it, pretty girl?"

"You," she quickly answers.

Drake and I are different in this aspect. I don't mind causing people pain, but not her. I want to kiss her and make everything better. My brother likes to cause pain to even her. And she wants it. I don't understand it, but I accept it. Although I wonder if the time will come when I get phased out. If Drake can give her everything she needs, why would she want me? She wouldn't. My brother might be enough for her, but I won't be. All three of my brothers mean the world to me. Then again, so does Natalia. What would I do if Drake decided he wanted her all to himself?

Chapter Thirty- Four

DRAKE

Today is the day. We're about to finally have all the puzzle's missing pieces. That is our sweet Natalia. She has been less than forthcoming with the information we want. I know her sister hates her, but I don't know why. Her parents have never tried to protect her, but I have no clue why. What could she have possibly done to make her own family have such distaste for her? I feel like it takes a lot of bullying to get to where the victim wants to cut their own flesh. I want to know everything. And we will get it or all three of them will pay with their lives. We let her sister go once without getting the answers we were seeking. It won't happen twice. Do I know how pissed she'd be if we went back on our word and killed the cunt? Yeah, but she'll get over it when she realizes she's better off without her. That's not family. She doesn't need people like that in her life. She needs us.

Dante is unusually quiet as we drive to the warehouse where the sister and parents wait for us. I turn onto the freeway and ask him, "What's up?"

He glances at me before continuing to gaze out the window. "Nothing."

I give him a few minutes before I press him again, "Dante. Spit it out."

My brother glances at me with a worried expression. "Are you planning to take her from me?"

"What?"

He shrugs his shoulders. "Sharing is fine for a while, right? But people don't do it forever. I assume eventually you'll decide you want her to yourself."

I chuckle loudly before rolling my eyes. "Ever heard the word polyamorous? People absolutely choose to do it forever. Aside from that, I am happy with how things are. And I'd never do that to you. You've got to know me better than that."

My brother has been in love with Natalia for a long time. I don't think she has any clue how deep his feelings run for her. But I do. While I might not be a good man, I am a good brother and I'd never hurt him like that. Stealing Natalia from him would be unforgivable.

"You're my brother. Trust me, I'd never do that to you. I don't think she'd go for it either. Why would you even think we would?"

He closes his eyes and throws his back against the seat. "You've got this pain thing. What do I have?"

I answer honestly, "Her heart."

That's the truth. I've had her body and I will have it again. I'll take her pain and her breath when I want it. But a man like me doesn't get a heart like Natalia's. I don't deserve it and I never will.

"Dante, this type of dynamic can work." It requires open and honest communication, but it doesn't have to be wrought with jealousy. There's no need for it.

She's ours. Not mine. Not yours. Ours."

My brother groans, "Alright. I'll get out of my head about it. I trust you."

After they were all brought to the warehouse, my guy asked if I wanted them together or separate. My initial thought was to keep them in different rooms, but I decided against it, hoping they'll feed on the others' fear.

I pull in behind the warehouse and park my truck, we both get out and nod to our security guy that mans the outside. The building is large and completely soundproof. There are rooms where we keep weapons and drugs, however nothing can be seen by the naked eye. Anything illegal is kept underground. Sometimes after we kill someone, Dante cleans it up and other times we bring in a cleaning crew. My brother is the most skilled out of all of us with cleaning up bloody messes. It's a skill he had no choice but to develop when Domenic decided he would do all the grunt work. Dante is my kid brother, and I never blamed him like Domenic did. When he was shot, nobody was more horrified than Dante. When Domenic makes up his mind about something, it's set in stone. He never backs away from a grudge. The only reason he mended things with Dante is because his wife, Giada, demanded it. She is the only person I've ever seen to influence my brother to do the right thing. She has turned my brother into a kinder, gentler madman. He's still lethal, but he is a little less of an asshole. That title is only owned by me now.

We walk into the room where all three of our victims are chained. The thick metal wraps around their wrists suspended over their heads. Each of them, attached to the ceiling and with a click of a button, can be raised or lowered, painfully.

Both Dante and I take a seat in front of our captives and simply stare at them. It's the woman that speaks first, Natalia's mother. According to Benji, her name is Bebe Grant. She never worked outside of the home. Her job was to stay home with her children, twin daughters, Natalia and Nicole, as well as their brother, Pax.

Bebe screams like she has any power here, "Let us go!"

We both chuckle at her ridiculousness, because surely she must know that will not happen. If she leaves here alive, it will be a miracle. Horrible things have happened to our girl and once I find out what those things are, we can make them right. Set her free from the demons that enslave her.

I hold the remote in my hand and raise Bebe just enough to cause a pull in her arms, making her scream, before I lower her back to the ground.

"Tell me about Natalia as a child."

She looks at me first with surprise and then fear, which quickly turns to obvious hatred. "That little bitch. Is that why we're here? I'll kill her myself."

Wrong fucking response. I raise her and leave her stretched painfully.

"Tell me about Natalia as a child. Be very careful. Bebe. I can cause far more pain than what you've experienced thus far."

Henry Grant stares at us with the fear of a little mouse being chased by a giant cat. "She liked ballet. It was all she thought about."

Dante says, "She grew out of that interest?"

Henry shakes his head. "No. There was an injury, and she never danced again."

I glance at Dante when he inquires further, "What kind of injury? Exactly what happened?"

Bebe says, "She was attacked. Someone took a bat to her knees when she was practicing for her debut as a ballerina."

I snort, "Someone Tanya Harding'd her. Who would do that?"

Body language can tell you a lot about a person. Henry glances at his daughter before hurrying his gaze elsewhere. It's Nicole that tells us the most with that hard swallow of her throat.

"You hit your sister with a bat?" I ask, unable to mask my surprise.

She shakes her head quickly. "No, of course not."

Dante is seconds away from attacking her, so I intervene. "I suggest you tell us the truth before my brother slices you from head to toe."

As if I had a great idea, my brother retrieves a knife from his pocket and sits with it in his hands as he gently strokes the tip of the blade like he's lost in the fantasy of the bloody murder he's dying to commit.

"I had my boyfriend do it."

My eyes dart between the three of them. "But why?"

The father attempts to shrug his shoulders as if it's no big fucking deal. "Sibling rivalry, I guess."

I'm familiar with sibling rivalry, but this isn't it. This goes far deeper than that. Sibling rivalry doesn't result in assault. Especially not something as brutal as this.

"It would appear that no one in your family likes Natalia. We don't understand why, but we want to."

Dante gets up and stands in front of Henry with the knife in his hand, not threatening exactly but reminding him why he should answer all questions.

"Why do you hate your daughter?" my brother asks, but of course answering isn't optional.

"She's not my daughter."

I'm getting a headache from this nonsense.

"Is Nicole not your daughter, either?"

Maybe that's it. Perhaps someone else is the biological father of these children.

He shakes his head. "Nicole is my daughter. Natalia is not."

Back to the confusing twin thing. Two twin sisters that don't even look like siblings. Nicole and Pax look related. Natalia looks like the adopted one out of the three of them.

I raise the mother's arms another couple of inches, resulting in her crying out in pain exactly how I intended, "Explain."

She begs, "Please let me down. It hur-hurts."

Chuckling, I lower her. "Explain faster. I'm losing my patience."

This time, she's quick to give me what I'm looking for. "Natalia isn't ours biologically."

Dante rubs at his temples, mirroring my state of mind. He says, "They are twins. Twins share the same parents."

Henry shakes his head. "They aren't twins. There's no blood relation between Natalia and any of us."

That explains why Natalia looks nothing like anybody in this family. However, it doesn't answer the biggest what the fuck question I have.

"How?"

They all glance at each other and Nicole screams, "Just tell them. If you don't, we are all dead. Tell them why you lied. Tell them why I had to pretend she was my sister for all these years."

I agree with Nicole because my patience is hanging on by a very thin thread. If that thread breaks, I'm going to kill all three of them before I get what I want.

I take a deep breath, attempting to steady my irritation that's growing with every second. "Why?"

Bebe stares between Dante and me, both with wide, terrified eyes. "I took her. Henry agreed to it because he didn't want me to go to prison. We said they were twins because we couldn't get a birth certificate for Natalia for obvious reasons. Since Nicole was born at home, we said I had twins. It was easier. Fewer questions."

Dante moves from Henry to Bebe and if I gave a fuck about this woman, I'd be concerned for her life right now. He holds the knife in front of her face as he screams, "You fucking kidnapped her? You aren't even her goddamn family?"

She nods slowly as she stares at the blade only a couple of inches from her face. "Y-y-yes," she stammers pitifully.

"I'm going to kill you so fucking slowly," my brother says calmly. Of course, I tell him he can't because we aren't done yet.

"And you knew?" I ask Nicole as I point to her. She nods. "I overheard them when I was little. I could have whatever I wanted as long as I never spoke about it."

Chapter Thirty-Five

DANTE

Normally when I end a life I'm not really pissed, it's simply what needs to be done, but now I'm more than pissed, I'm furious and the rage is intense. They kidnapped our girl and treated her like absolute shit. Made her fucking hate herself so much that she cuts her own beautiful skin. As usual, Drake saves me from losing my mind and acting without thinking things through.

"Dante, let's go. We need to talk to her. She'll never believe this if she doesn't hear it from these assholes herself."

Natalia. This is about her, not my selfish need to bleed all three of them out. I nod, put my knife away, and follow him out. He stops and tells our security team to separate the three future murder victims.

"I don't want them to have the opportunity to talk. Each of them is to be held in separate rooms. Make sure they have food and water. I can't have anything happening until we are ready."

Once we step out into the fresh air, I take a deep, cleansing breath. "Fuck. This is going to kill her."

He snorts as he opens the truck door. "No fucking kidding. I'm going to be on razor blade watch 24/7."

We both get in the truck and, thinking out loud, I say, "That still doesn't explain why Nicole hates her so much."

Drake chuckles as he puts the truck into drive and peels out of the parking lot. "We will take care of everything, little brother, but we need to talk to Domenic."

I glance at him like he's truly lost his mind, because I'm pretty sure he has. If we tell him how we got here, how we came to find out this information, he's going to go ballistic. I'm not worried about my brother hitting me or killing me. He might kick the shit out of me, but I can handle that. Not being his family again. That's not something I can stomach.

Drake drives toward Domenic's house and sighs, "It'll be fine. We did nothing worse than what he did with his wife."

He's not entirely wrong. However, the way Domenic will see it is that he kidnapped Giada because she was a threat to our family. Natalia isn't a fucking threat to anyone. She's good. And doesn't come from a rival family. Instead, she comes from a family of psychotic kidnappers. Jesus Christ.

Drake calls Domenic on speaker phone as we approach the neighborhood he lives in. He answers quickly, and Drake says, "We need a family meeting. It's urgent."

We never speak about business over the phone, so he doesn't even question it. He only responds with, "Damian is here. I assume Dante is with you?"

I answer for him, "I am. We're about ten minutes out."

After I hit the button on the stereo controls to end the call, we drive the rest of the way in silence. I'm less worried about my other brother's reactions to what Drake and I have been up to. My primary concern is Natalia. Her mental health always feels like she's on the edge of completely crumbling. This information may be too much for her to take. We know she attempted suicide more than once in her teenage years. That's what concerns me, her deciding She has nothing to live for. Right now, things are bad with her so-called family, but she lives for some magical sister relationship she craves. If we take that from her, what then? Her world is about to be turned upside down. We will be the two men that pulled the rug from underneath her and in complete and utter devastation. Sure, we aren't the assholes that did this to her, but will she hold us responsible, considering without her she may have never known the truth?

As if he can read my mind, he says, "She'll be alright. We'll be sure of it."

I'm not sure I share my brother's positivity, but I know she has the fucking right to know her entire life is a lie. This is how she gets these abusive monsters out of her life. We pull up to our normal parking spot outside of Domenic's place and silently step outside of the vehicle. As we walk up the steps to the door, Drake says, "Everything is going to change, but she's still ours. No matter what anyone says. Including Natalia."

I don't respond, but I don't have to. Drake knows well that I have no intention of ever setting her free. Even if it's the right thing to do, I could never bring myself to do it. We walk through the house and, of course, stop out to the pool area where we know we'll find our girl and her best friend. Natalia looks stunning in a dark blue two piece that shows off every fucking inch of those delicious curves I've gotten to know so well. She flashes us a shy smile as she looks at Giada with an unsure glance. Drake saves us from being too suspicious. "I wanted to see how my nephew is."

Giada laughs as she rubs her large belly. "Stubborn. Still in here. Did you hear we got an induction date?"

"We did. I'm sure you'll be glad to not be pregnant anymore."

Domenic has said that she's been fairly pleasant during her pregnancy, but she's been uncomfortable for the last few weeks and he'll be glad it's over with. He hates seeing her miserable. Apparently, she can't get any rest at night because the baby keeps her up with relentless kicking. I can't help but wonder what Natalia would look like with that swollen baby bump. I don't even know if she wants children. For that matter, I don't really know if my brother or I do either. And how would that work? Would we both be dad? Or would we find out the paternity and one would be dad while the other is uncle? Drake pulls me out of my thoughts. "It was good seeing you, ladies. We have a meeting with Domenic and Damian."

As we walk back inside, we can hear the two women giggling. Drake chuckles as he shakes his head. "That woman."

We make it up to Domenic's office and find Damian sitting in the chair across from his desk. Drake and I grab a seat on the black leather sofa sitting to the side of the room. Our brother doesn't take much time. He gets right to business. "What's the urgent matter?"

I pinch the bridge of my nose. "It's a long story, but try to hear us out before reacting. Natalia's sister stole from us. That's how it started."

Drake and I take turns filling them both in on everything that has transpired, including the fact that we're holding the three of them in the warehouse and everything Natalia doesn't even know about herself.

Domenic slams his fist down on the desk. "You kidnapped my wife's best friend!"

Drake shrugs like it's not a big deal. "No. You kidnapped your wife. We coerced her best friend."

While they argue about who committed the bigger crime, Damian laughs like a maniac. I raise an eyebrow in question. "Something funny?"

Once he regains composure, he grins, "My brothers are all psychopaths. Can you not get dates without taking fucking hostages?"

Drake leans forward with his elbows on his knees and glares at Damian with a heated expression. "We did not kidnap her."

Domenic drags his hand down his face in exasperation, "Alright. So what's the plan?"

Drake stands, signaling that he's done with this conversation. "We will tell Natalia and handle the three people in the warehouse. I just wanted you to know because I'm imagining this will be a tough pill for her to swallow. Although you're expecting a baby soon, she will probably need Giada. I'm not sure how much she's going to let us help her."

Domenic shakes his head at me in disgust, "You just couldn't leave her alone?"

My response is simple and true, "No more than you could leave Giada alone."

Drake and I walk to the door and I turn back to Domenic. "We're taking her with us. You should be prepared to answer your wife's questions."

We make it back downstairs and find Natalia and Giada giggling in the kitchen about baby names. Drake grabs her hand and pulls her away from our sister-in-law. "Come on, pretty girl. It's time to go."

"My car," she complains, but Drake shakes his head, telling her not to argue. "We'll have it brought home."

Giada looks at Natalia and I know our girl hasn't said a word when Giada's mouth forms an 'O' from shock as a few pieces of the puzzle slide into place for her. As Drake pulls Natalia to the front door, her friend yells, "Text me!"

She walks with Drake in front of me, and my eyes can't help but focus on the swaying of her full hips as she steps closer to the vehicle.

"Sunshine."

Natalia stops and turns to me. I motion for her to come to me and she does. Taking her face in my hands, I lower my head and press my lips to hers. She grabs onto my shirt, fists it and pulls me closer as I push my tongue into her mouth. A little moan slips out of her and speaks directly to my cock.

Drake growls loudly, "Let's go, you two."

Chapter Thirty-Six

NATALIA

The ride back to the house was quiet. I could tell both men had something on their minds, but they didn't tell me what it was. I didn't ask because it felt wrong. The air was thick with anxiety and I think I was almost afraid if I questioned it, they'd tell me the truth. Whatever the truth is, I'm not sure I want to know about it. As soon as we walk into the house, Drake says, "Sit," while pointing at the sectional. I take a seat and wait while the wheels in my head keep turning, and it finally hits me.

They've had their fill. Both men are done with me and want me to leave. This is what I wanted, right? Why is the lump in my throat growing? Why am I ready to cry when I never wanted either of these men to begin with?

I shake my head, trying to keep my emotions at bay. "You don't have to say anything. I'll go."

Drake folds his arms over his chest as he narrows his gaze at me. "What?"

I wipe a tear that breaks free. "We don't need to have a conversation. You're done. I'll go."

He chuckles with amusement, "You aren't going anywhere, pretty girl. We are nowhere near done with you, but we need to have a conversation. It's going to be hard to hear, but it's necessary."

Dante kneels in front of me, "Sunshine. Your parents aren't your parents."

"What?" I ask because I heard the words he said, but they make little sense to me, so I'm sure I've misheard him.

"They aren't your biological parents," Drake clarifies.

I laugh because for years I fantasized I had been adopted and my real parents were looking for me. Reality eventually squashed the fantasy, just like it does with all fantasies. I hadn't been adopted and nobody that loved me fiercely was looking for me.

I glance at Dante first and then Drake; both expressions show concern but I still don't understand what they're trying to say.

"What are you talking about?"

Drake says, "Bebe kidnapped you when you were a baby. Those assholes are not your family."

I gasp loudly before asking, "They kidnapped us?"

Dante squeezes my hand gently. "No sunshine. Just you. She isn't your sister."

Drake approaches us and says, "It's time to go see them. They will answer every single question you have."

Pushing away from Dante, I rise from my seat, "I am not going to my parent's house."

Both brothers grab one of my hands as Drake says, "No. We are going to our warehouse, where they are being held."

My eyes snap to his. "You kidnapped them?"

He chuckles like I told a funny joke, "After what they've done to you, they are lucky to be still breathing. Although, the only reason they aren't dead is so that you can get the answers you need."

What game are these two playing? This can't possibly be true. My family hates me. Indeed, had they kidnapped me they would've returned me because none of them can stand the sight of me. Their hatred for me runs so deep that I'm sure if this were true I w, would've been back with my biological family within years.

"Is this a cruel joke?"

I don't get a response from either brother. Instead, I'm pulled out of the house and back to the car. I sit in the back with a man on each side of me. Drake grabs my leg, but I glare at him. "Don't fucking touch me."

Much to my surprise, he listened and removed his hand from my leg. "For now, pretty girl. For now, I'll let you be in charge. Just don't get used to it because you're mine. I have no intention of not touching my property."

I roll my eyes at him, "People are not possessions, Drake. You don't own me. Neither of you do."

He grips my chin tight and watches me with apparent interest. "Pretty girl, I will possess you. Every part of you won't be able to exist without us. I'll be sure of it. We own you, Natalia. One day soon, you'll be thankful for that fact."

"I hate you," I whisper. I want to hurt him, but it only makes him laugh.

"You want to, baby. You've tried, but you can't because nobody gives you everything you need like I do. No other man can feel your pain. No other man knows how to take that pain away. Both my brother and I can give you everything you've never even known that you needed."

I struggle out of his grip, and he allows it as I turn away from him. "You're such an asshole."

My emotions are all over the place. With every second that we drive, it gets harder to breathe. I'm pissed at them both, but I'm not sure why. Because they blackmailed me into this bizarre situation? Maybe because they are lying to me about my family? Perhaps it's the false hope that I'll finally get the answer to the biggest question of my life.

Why does my family hate me so much?

Your blood is supposed to love you simply because you share blood. It's not complicated. There's no doubt about it. It just is. For my entire life, I've never fit. It's like trying to fit a square peg into a round hole. I'm the square peg. The one piece that doesn't belong. I once read that the need for belonging is the reason cults are born. Because everybody wants to find that place where they are accepted for who they are. They want to find their people. Giada is the closest I've ever found. She loves me despite all my flaws, and there are many. Now that she's married, it's different. It'll probably change even more after she's a mother. I'm happy for her. I'm just really unhappy for myself.

Of course, I want all the good things for my best friend. Is it too much to ask to have a little positive thrown my way too? Yeah, I'm sulking. I need to snap out of this and deal with the issue at hand. My family.

I still can't wrap my head around what these two jerks could gain by lying to me about this. What is it they're after? Maybe they want to hurt me by hurting my family? That thought causes bile to rise in my throat, but it's the only thing that makes any sense to me. It's more sensible than the alternative that they are telling the truth.

Stop it Natalia. They are liars. If it's unbelievable, it's because it's fiction.

Chapter Thirty-Seven

DRAKE

Her conflicted emotions become apparent as we pull up to the warehouse where her kidnappers await for our return. I know well that Natalia doesn't believe a fucking word we said about Bebe kidnapping her from her biological parents. I can't say that I blame her. If she came to me and said my mother had kidnapped me, I wouldn't believe her either. Although, you can tell by looking at my brothers that we're all related. When I first saw Nicole, I knew they didn't look like sisters, but I never would've imagined the true story.

Both Dante and I take one of her hands and walk inside. We take her to see Bebe first because, of course, she's the one who set this ball in motion by stealing her. Our security team stands close by but far enough away to give us privacy. My brother and I will only have to say the word to get their help, but we likely won't need it unless we decide to have them kill one or all of these pieces of shit. However, I don't see that happening because this is one I want to handle personally, and I suspect Dante feels the same way.

She steps into the room and stares at the woman she believes is her mother. Exhaling a shaky gasp, she asks, "Is this really necessary?"

Between the two of us, my brother is the better man. However, he's a lethal fucker like the rest of us. And that these people have hurt Natalia so badly means there's no way that any of them will be granted any mercy. Even if I agreed to let them live, Dante will not. Not even for Natalia.

She looks at Dante with tears in her eyes. "Dante, please."

I chuckle lightly because I know my brother better than she does. He loves her and wants to make her happy, but we both know in time, this will be exactly what she needs. We don't allow people to hurt the ones we care about and leave unscathed.

He runs his thumb down her cheek. "Get the information you need, sunshine."

"Mom," she asks as she steps closer to Bebe, who stares at her supposed daughter with disgust. I clench my fists as she looks at our girl like she's a piece of disgusting shit on the floor. Dante growls a deep rumbling animalistic sound, "Close enough."

Natalia stops, balling up her own fists, in obvious anger. She takes a deep breath. "Mom. Are you okay?"

Bebe glares at her. "Stop calling me that. I'm not your mother, and we both know it."

I watch the two of them as our beautiful woman visibly shrinks before us. "I don't understand."

Dante grabs a chair and brings it over to Natalia. "Sit."

She sits in the chair and my brother tells Bebe, "Spill. Everything."

At first she says nothing, but when I hold up the remote she stammers, "Okay. Okay."

I chuckle and motion for her to move it along because the sooner we get this shit over with, the sooner we can glue Natalia back together.

"After Nicole was born, I wanted another little girl. I couldn't get pregnant again because I had to have an emergency hysterectomy within hours of her birth."

Natalia listens intently, but I know she's confused. "Go on," she says.

Bebe tries to move her arms, but of course it's not possible. She groans in pain, saying, "It was at Walt Disney World." Your mother fell to the ground during some kind of medical emergency. Without thinking about it, I grabbed your stroller and took off with you as people ran to help her. I was gone before anyone noticed you were missing. Henry never wanted you, but he knew if I returned you, I'd go to prison. So we kept you. Even after we realized you would never fit in with our family. It was like constantly playing a game of which of these things does not belong. At that point, we were stuck with you."

"Is my mother alive?" Natalia asks in the smallest voice I think I've ever heard her use.

Bebe laughs, "I don't know. Honestly, I don't even know her name."

"Anything else, Sunshine?" Dante asks.

She shakes her head, "No. Wait. Yes. Why did you take me?"

"I thought you were the missing piece I wanted. You weren't. I've regretted it every day since I brought you into our lives. Now, tell these assholes to let me go."

Stepping forward, I watch my new favorite fucking sight. I've been waiting for Natalia to stand up for herself. To stop acting like a goddamn doormat. She glares at Bebe with a fierce expression. "No. If they kill you, my only request will be to watch."

Turning to me, she smiles, "I'm ready to see Nicole now."

NATALIA

I hold my head high and walk out of the room, ignoring her vile words. In the middle of a deep, cleansing breath, Drake grabs me by the throat and pushes me up against the wall. "Jesus Christ, pretty girl. I knew one day you'd show us how fucking strong you are."

A whimper escapes from my mouth as his lips descend on mine. Dante groans while he watches his brother practically fuck my mouth with his tongue. Drake breaks our kiss with a chuckle. "Are you ready, baby?"

I nod breathlessly because I'm ready to get this over with. Neither of my so-called parents have been kind to me through the years. However, no one has been more vicious than Nicole. She has always been my biggest tormentor. The voice in my head telling me how worthless I am is hers. I have taken it for years, hoping she'd one day mature and realize what a monster she has been and things would magically change. I longed for a sister, that relationship you hear about between siblings. To find out she's not even related to me is mind-boggling.

"I need to find my parents," I say to both brothers as we walk into the room where Nicole is being held.

Dante assures me, "I'm on it," while I observe Nicole, her arms chained above her head, just like Bebe. I have always been a good person. I try to do the right thing. I'm not one of those people that go out of my way to hurt people. *Unlike Nicole.*

Yet here I am, staring at her miserable face, tears streaking her cheeks, and instead of feeling bad for her, I think I might be elated. Yes, I'm taking joy in her misfortune. For once, I have the upper hand.

Drake says, "Do you have questions for her, baby?"

There is one burning question I've had for years. It's stupid because I already know the answer, but I want to hear it from her spiteful mouth.

"It was you, right? You're the reason I can't dance."

As always, she denies it, "I didn't touch your knees."

I glance at Drake, since Dante appears to be busy texting on his phone.

"Can you make her tell me the truth?"

He grins in response. "I thought you'd never ask."

Pulling a remote from his pocket, he presses a button and Nicole screams as her arms are pulled up, the chains on her wrists moving further up to the ceiling. Interesting.

"I know it wasn't you that hit me, but you're responsible for it, right?"

She hangs from the ceiling, her feet just above the floor, and I know her arms hurt as she's being unnaturally stretched.

"Yes. I had him do it."

Drake says to me, "Do you want her to tell you why?"

I shake my head, "No. I already know the answer to that. Nicole was never as good of a dancer as I was. The only way she could dance the lead was to take me out."

Dante pockets his phone and asks me, "What else do you need, Sunshine?"

"A bat. I need a bat."

Drake arches an eyebrow. "We don't have a bat. How about a hammer?"

I glare at him with the anger I'm feeling for Nicole. "I need a bat."

A delicious smirk forms on his lips as he pulls out his cell phone. "Alright, pretty girl. We will get you a bat."

I smile at Nicole, "While we wait, tell me why."

She stares at me through her reddened eyes. "Why what?"

Crossing my arms over my chest, I shake my head. "Don't play coy. Why do you hate me so much? Our entire lives, you've done everything you can to hurt me. I want to know why."

Nicole releases a shaky breath, "I don't know. Mom hated you, so I guess I did, too."

I laugh bitterly, "Your mother kidnapped me. And it's me you hated? Did you ever consider hating her? She's the one who did this. If it weren't for her, I wouldn't have ever met you."

When Nicole cries, I wonder if it's an act or if it's an honest emotion. With her, you never really know because she's always so manipulative. "I hated you because you were better than me at everything. You danced better. Played piano better. Got better grades. Every single thing. It drove me crazy, so when Mom suggested I take your ability to dance, I ran with it. I'm sorry. Please don't let them hurt me."

Moving closer to her, I forcefully grab her face and squeeze it, just like her mother did to do to me countless times. "I won't let them hurt you. I promise."

"Thank you," she whispers, "Thank you."

I laugh wickedly. Right now, I don't know who I am, but I know she drove me to this. "I will do it myself. For every tear I cried after you destroyed me time and time again, you'll cry twice as much. The pain will be excruciating. Yet, while I did nothing to you, I never deserved what you did to me. You will. Remember that when you're crying, 'why me?' you did this to yourself.

Chapter Thirty-Eight

DANTE

This is not how either of us expected her to handle this day. Both of us expected her to be emotional and more than a little broken to find out her truth. We wouldn't have thought less of her for that type of reaction. I think most women would break down with the information Natalia has gotten today. Yet she's not any woman. She's ours. Even when we found out she was cutting herself, we still knew this strength and resilience were inside of her the entire time. Cutting didn't make her weak. We don't like it and won't allow it, but we also don't judge her for it. She did what she had to in order to survive. But it's our job to help her find other ways to release that pain. We will never stop her from expressing herself, but only if she does it safely.

Our newest guy, Brandon, comes running in with a bat and tries to hand it to him, but I narrow my gaze at him. "Hand it to Natalia."

He does not know who she is but obviously can figure out that it's not the chained up woman. Brandon gives her the bat and flashes me a weary look and walks out of the room. He has worked for us for about four months, but nobody that works for us has ever seen a woman handing out punishments. They also don't know what these people did to gain entry to our warehouse. They don't need to know her story. Unless she tells it, no one outside of our family will ever know.

Natalia rubs the length of the bat as she smiles at Nicole. "This is probably gonna sting."

I knew she had strength in her, but this crazy side surprises me. No, it delights me. Now there's no doubt. She's perfect for us.

Pretty little psycho.

Clearly she wants to do this, but I wonder if she'll be able to swing the bat. Wanting to hurt someone and being able to actually do it are two very different things. Turning around, she glances back at us like she was making sure she wouldn't accidentally hit us. She smiles slightly. "Stay back."

Fuck. Natalia taking control like this is the hottest thing I've ever gotten to witness. She turns back to Nicole, who is trembling uncontrollably. Natalia pulls the bat back and swings it, hitting her left knee. I'm not sure which is louder, the crunching sound of bones or the blood-curdling screams Nicole yells out.

Our sweet girl pulls the bat back again before striking her other knee. But she doesn't stop. All her anger has been bottled up for years. It's as if someone unscrewed the cap and it's all coming rushing out like lava in a volcano.

Natalia stands in front of Nicole who continues to cry and whimper endlessly, our girl looks like the sexiest executioner as she raises the bat over her head, my brother and I watch with our full attention as Natalia says what will be the last words Nicole ever hears, "Fuck you."

The bat comes crashing down on her head. Blood and bits of her brain fly in different directions. Natalia drops the weapon at her feet and falls to the floor with a gut wrenching sob.

Drake says to me, "Get her showered and home. I'll have Brandon grab some clothes for her. I'll take care of the rest here and be there when I'm done."

I walk over to her and bend down, lifting her into my arms. I tell her the plan, and she looks up at Drake. "You aren't coming with us?"

He shakes his head. "Not right now, pretty girl. I'm going to take care of things here, but then I'll be home. What you need right now is Dante. He will take care of you."

There's an unspoken understanding between us I hadn't even realized existed until now. This is what Drake meant when he said I had her heart, although I don't completely agree because she has feelings for him as well. Although I can now clearly see that we both offer her different things. I think she needs both of us. I carry her off to the shower and set her on the counter. She stares at me with concern, and when I ask what's wrong, her response stuns me, nearly speechless.

"Do you see me differently now?"

I gaze at her in confusion. "What?"

Helping her out of her clothes, she speaks quietly, barely above a whisper, "I murdered her. I'm not the sweet girl you thought I was. Do you see me differently now?"

Lifting her so she's standing, I kneel before her, and undo her jeans before pulling them down her legs along with her panties.

Natalia, you're still my sunshine, the greatest thing ever to enter my life, and you'll always be my perfect sweet girl.

Once she's naked, I rise to my full height, grab her chin gently, as I stare at her bloody face. "She deserved it. They all do. Do not waste any energy on feeling guilty. She took so much from you and doesn't get to take anymore."

Moving away from her, I turn the water on, and once I have the water right, I tell her to step inside the shower. She does, and I get undressed so I can join her.

NATALIA

I quickly scrub my face and neck because the stench of Nicole's blood on my skin isn't something I want around. Dante steps in behind me and wraps his arms around me, pulling me tight against his chest, "I'm proud of you, sunshine."

Turning around to face him, I laugh lightly, "You're proud of me for killing someone?"

He narrows his gaze and says, "No. I'm proud of you for taking control of your life. I'm proud of you for destroying a person who would have kept hurting you until she took her final breath."

Nothing has turned out like I expected. Not with the brothers and definitely not with the people I thought were my family. Somehow it feels right, and that terrifies me.

Dragging my fingers up his chest, I do something far scarier than ending Nicole's life.

"Are you going to let me go now?"

He stares at me with a heated expression for what feels like an eternity before asking, "Is that what you want? Is that what you dream about? Being free of us?"

I shake my head no because it's the last thing I want. "I never wanted this. You both forced it on me with no thought of what it would mean for me. I should want to be free of you, but I don't. Lately I live every day wondering if today will be the day you tire of me and walk away."

He grabs my ass and lifts me effortlessly before slamming into me. "I'll never be tired of you. I'll never let you go. Not even if you beg me to."

I wrap my arms around his neck as he thrusts into me. Our wet skin sticks together as he grips my ass in a tight hold. I say the words I've never said to anyone, "Dante. I love you."

He paused with wide eyes before slamming my back against the shower wall. "Fuck. Sunshine. Jesus."

Taking my lips in an aggressive kiss, he continues fucking me like it's the first time. Sex with Dante and Drake is never bad. But it feels different this time, like it's more than sex. His gaze connects with mine and he demands, "Say it again."

Wrapping my legs tight around his waist, I speak my truth. "I love you. Dante, I love you."

He closes his eyes tight as if he's in pain. "I love you too, Natalia."

"Dante," I moan when he pulls out of me most of the way and slams back inside my pussy repeatedly.

"Come for me, baby."

My body pulses around him as I tremble. Consumed by an orgasm, I dig my nails into his back, completely lost in him. And it's perfect as I feel him come inside me. The only thing missing is his brother. I should be ashamed of myself, but I'm not. Finally, I can admit the truth to myself. I want both of them, and I only hope that Drake still wants me. I don't want either of them to walk away. If either of them didn't want me, it'd leave a gaping hole in my chest. One that I'm not sure would ever heal.

Chapter Thirty-Nine

DRAKE

It's amazing what you can find out from people that are trying to save their pathetic lives. Henry Grant told me it was August 4, 1998, when his wife came home with a baby that did not belong to her. He believes she was approximately three months old, but of course, they aren't sure when she was born. It was then that it occurred to me that our girl doesn't know when her birthday is or what her fucking name is. Natalia is a name Bebe chose because she thought it went with Nicole. And of course twins have to have names that start with the same letter. Benji is working on trying to find families that reported the kidnapping of infants in Orlando, Florida, in August of ninety-eight. If her mother was having a medical emergency when she was taken, it's possible she's dead. If her parents reported her as missing, which I'm sure they did, it shouldn't be difficult for Benji to find them. There's few people more skilled than he is with locating people.

After they left, I had sent a text to Dante telling him to make sure she gets rest because once I get home she'll be getting no sleep. I'm sure he fucked her several times after they got home and I'd bet my life that he comforted her with his dick while they were in the shower, so when I make it to the house, I'm taking my turn. I wanted to fuck her after she killed that bitch, but I knew she needed tenderness in that moment. That's Dante, not me. I'm not capable of being gentle.

After taking a quick shower by myself, yeah, I might be a little irritated by that. I get dressed and head out to my truck. Glancing at the clock on the stereo, I notice it's one in the morning. Our girl is probably sleeping, which is fine. I have no problem waking her with my tongue. Luckily the traffic is light at this time of night because my cock has been hard the entire drive home. I haven't been able to think of anything other than our girl writhing beneath me. The way she looks, her scent, her pussy gripping me, it's all perfection. But the way she sounds when she cries out my name, every fucking time, it's my undoing. I don't really understand it because that's never been what turns me on with a woman.

I pull into the driveway, after turning my truck off, I get out and make my way inside. Throwing my keys on the table near the stairs, I immediately go upstairs to find her, my greatest need.

As I suspected, I find her sleeping with my brother when I walk into the bedroom. I stare at her naked form while I get undressed. She looks stunning with her head on Dante's chest, her leg draped over his abdomen, her beautiful pussy on display for me. Her dark hair is splayed all over the place, confirming my thoughts that he had his fun

186

with her before she went to sleep. I drape my clothes over the chair before climbing on the bed and moving her to her back. After parting her legs, I lower my head and take her clit between my lips and suck. Even though she's asleep, she reacts immediately, moaning and thrusting her hips, pushing her pussy further into my face. My eyes take in her gorgeous body as my gaze creeps up to her hard little nipples, and then her face. Her eyes stay shut but her lips are slightly parted as she moans my name like she knows it's me even in her sleep. I suck harder, and her beautiful eyes pop open on a gasp, "Drake," she says as she grabs a hold of my hair. My brother watches her face as she moans for me.

"Did Dante make you sore tonight, baby?" I ask as I crawl up her body.

"A little, but please, I need you."

I chuckle as I drag my cock through her folds. "Such a greedy little pussy. This is why you're perfect for us, pretty girl. I'm not sure one man would be enough to satisfy you."

Leaning down, I drag my tongue over her nipple slowly, causing her to whine. She likes it best when I flick at her nipples quickly; she hates the slow the torture.

"Drake," she groans and I respond by biting her nipple hard, making her yelp.

"Who's in charge of this beautiful body, Natalia?"

"You," she pants like the needy little thing she is.

Holding myself up with a hand on either side of her on the mattress, I say, "Good girl."

I sit back on my knees, and push her thighs back and slide into her with a groan, "Fuck. I love this perfect body."

She arches an unapproving eyebrow, "I'm one hundred eighty pounds. My body is not perfect. It's fat."

For a moment, I stop moving and glare at her. That pissed me off. I don't like anyone talking about her like that, not even herself.

"I don't give a fuck what the scale says, pretty girl. To us, you are complete perfection. Talk like that again and you will be punished. You don't have a single curve out of place. Nothing is too much or too little. You're exactly right."

I don't take my eyes from hers as I address my brother. "Dante, I think our beautiful girl needs a reminder of what it's like to be worshiped by two men."

NATALIA

Dante kneels beside me and kisses me while his brother fucks me. His tongue swirls around mine, almost in a pornographic way. It's slow, sensual and nearly causes me to lose my mind. Drake digs his fingers into my thighs as he pounds into me. Dante grabs my bouncing breasts with a growl and squeezes my nipples. Dante's tongue travels down my neck, straight to my breasts, licking my nipples like he does my clit with fast, firm strokes. I dig my fingers into his hair while I run my fingers down Drake's chest with my free hand. It all becomes so much sensation with Drake's dick inside me and Dante's mouth practically eating me alive. The pleasure is too intense.

"Come for us, pretty girl."

I shake my head. "I can't. No. I can't."

He chuckles, "You can. And you will. Let go."

Drake reaches between my legs and pinches my clit hard, causing me to first scream and then explode with an orgasm that causes me to yell even louder.

Dante grabs my face, "So fucking beautiful, baby. My brother is right. You're perfect. For us."

The emotion in my chest almost becomes too much as Drake finishes inside me before collapsing beside me. I had never even fantasized about being with two men. It wasn't something that held any interest for me. But these two men, two totally different sides of the same coin, do things to me I never want to end. Good things always have to end though, right? Every story must have an ending. The only question is whether this one will have a tragic one that will leave me in complete destruction.

Chapter Forty

DRAKE

I was sure I could feel nothing for a woman, but after last night, I know I was wrong. The need to protect Natalia and make sure she has everything she's ever wanted is fierce. After I finished dealing with her kidnappers, I couldn't get home fast enough to her. It was my only thought. My brother is my best friend and with Natalia, things somehow feel complete. Both Dante and I work in sync in the kitchen, making breakfast for our girl. We have Benji working on the list of people that had babies go missing in 1998. This is all part of our need to give her everything in life. She was ripped from her family before she got to know them. We will rectify that best as we can. Dante and I have already discussed that no one will meet her without doing a DNA test first because we don't want to watch her break from disappointment.

I spot my brother glaring over my shoulder, so I turn around to find Natalia standing there with a duffel bag over her shoulder and her purse in her hand.

"What the fuck is this?" I ask.

She shrugs nonchalantly. "I figured Nicole was dead, so I'll get out of your hair. I'm going to stay with Giada until I can find a new place to live."

Everything stops. I swallow hard as I try to regain the ability to form words.

"You're leaving us?" My brother asks, since I've apparently lost the ability to speak.

She nods as she fingers the straps on her duffle bag. "Yeah. You know, while the memories are good. Before everything gets messy."

I motion for her to come over to me and, much to my surprise, she does. She stands in front of me, her beautiful lashes fluttering lightly as she lifts her gaze to mine.

"You aren't leaving, pretty girl. As much as I don't delight in holding you hostage, I will. Neither of us is prepared to watch you walk away."

"Drake," she says in a whisper, "I can't stay. I'm afraid."

She's running scared.

"The only way to get through fear is to walk through it."

Her eyes dart between Dante and me. "How long can things last like this? Will I be made to choose? I couldn't. It'd be an impossible choice."

I take her face in my hands and stare at her as I take in her beautiful features, "Why choose, pretty girl? We aren't asking you to. We don't want you to. You have two men that want to keep you permanently and give you everything you've ever wanted. The only choice you have to make is whether or not you're here consensually. I promise you, no matter what, you aren't leaving. You're ours. Time won't change that. Nothing will."

Unshed tears fill her eyes as she tries to blink them away. "I don't want to go, but I don't want to stay and wait for you to kick me out."

"Pretty girl, I don't know how to make it any more clear to you. Nobody is going anywhere. You want one of us to marry you? Give you a fucking house full of babies? Guaranteed, my brother will do it in a heartbeat."

She jerks away from me and I let her go, "I know Dante loves me, he told me. I'm not worried about losing him. It's you. Losing either of you would be a cut so deep I'd never recover."

I could just tell her she's not leaving, end of the conversation, but I don't want it to be that way if it doesn't have to be. My brother is watching me like I'm the person standing between him and the puppy he's always wanted. I ignore him and focus on her. "What do you need, Natalia? What do you want from me?"

She storms toward me, slams her fists into my chest and screams, "I want to fucking matter. I want to be enough for both of you."

Dante says, "She wants you to say you love her."

I glance at my brother, "Call Nico," and grab her wrists, pulling her close to me.

"Baby, I'm not a word guy. I'll never write you fucking poetry comparing your hair to the sun. You do matter. You are enough for us. Pretty girl, you're fucking everything. When Nico gets here and tattoos your name on my fucking dick, maybe then you'll see there's only one woman I want. This is not temporary. It's permanent."

She looks up at me and giggles, "Nobody would ever write poetry and compare my hair to the sun. My hair is dark, and the sun is yellow. And tattooing your dick? You really are a psycho, Drake."

Leaning down, I bite her lip, drawing blood, and lick the coppery taste from her. "I'm the same psycho that's going to spank your ass for the attitude you're giving me, pretty girl."

Dante's phone chimes and he says, "Shit. Giada is in labor. We have to go."

Natalia grins at me like she won a contest. "Saved by the bell."

"Don't worry, baby. I'll get that ass later in a way you won't see coming."

Of course, she does not know what I'm talking about and once she does, it'll be too late.

NATALIA

I'm not the woman that's dying to have babies. In fact, I've never wanted children. I'm excited for my best friend to become a mom because she wants it desperately. I've just never seen the draw to it. Maybe it has something to do with my upbringing. Bebe certainly didn't seem to enjoy having children. Even Pax and Nicole seemed to annoy her endlessly. While she didn't hate them like me, I wouldn't say she was warm with them either. Some people should not be allowed to procreate. I think I'd be a shit mom, so when Drake offered to fill the house with babies, that's not what I wanted. It's why I have an implant for birth control. I'm curious about how Giada's baby will affect me. I've never even held a baby before and I wonder if some maternal need will kick in after their baby is born.

It warms my heart that she was asking for me, even though she has Domenic there with her. Maybe things won't change as much as I've feared they will. Drake is driving the truck while I sit in the middle between my two men. I gasp when Dante reaches his hand under my shirt and rubs his thumb over the thin fabric covering my nipple. Leaning down, he sucks on my neck while his hand causes wetness to pool in my panties.

"Dante."

He groans in my ear, "Are you going to be a good girl and come like this for me?"

I whimper, "I don't know if I can."

Drake complains, "Why am I always stuck with driving duty?"

He turns slightly and begins teasing both my nipples, making me writhe in my seat. "That's our girl. Come for us."

I've always had sensitive breasts but I've never come just from them being played with. I didn't even think it was possible to orgasm that way, but when he flicks both of them with quick little swipes of his thumbs, I know that's exactly what's going to happen.

"Dante."

The truck pulls to a stop and Dante's mouth devours the right side of my neck, while his brother does the same on my left. It's the growl that vibrates through Drake's chest that does me in. "Come on, pretty girl. Show us how beautiful you are when you come."

With their tongues on my skin, Dante's thumbs stimulating my nipples and the filthy talk, I lose myself in the sensation.

"Drake. Dante," I moan louder than I should have in the hospital underground parking garage.

First Dante kisses me slowly before his brother grabs my face, turns me to him and slams his lips to mine aggressively, licking inside my mouth like a starving man.

He pulls away from me reluctantly. "Let's get this over with so I can punish that beautiful ass."

I gasp lightly. "I thought you might forget."

Drake chuckles as he steps out of the truck. "Not a chance, pretty girl. When I'm old and gray and can't remember why I stepped into a room, I'll still remember to spank your disobedient ass."

Drake takes my left hand in his while Dante takes my right as we walk into the hospital to see Gia. I'm sure people are looking at us and wondering what this strange dynamic is because it's also strange to me. It might be different, something I never would've expected, but also I've never in my entire life been so happy, felt so protected. I don't know what the future holds with these two dangerous men and I'm still terrified, but there's no place I'd rather be.

Chapter Forty-One

DANTE

After sixteen hours of labor, Giada finally gave birth to a baby boy. Domenic Jr. weighed in at a whopping eleven pounds, which is surprising given how tiny Giada is. However, my brother is six-foot-six, so it's likely his son will also be big.

Of course, I've thought about Natalia being pregnant. She'd be so hot I'd want to be inside her constantly. Watching her hold my nephew has only increased my interest. Drake and I both watch closely as the two women go on about how good he smells. That's strange, right?

The baby is a spitting image of my brother, dark velvety hair, and dark eyes. It makes me wonder what our baby would look like. Then again, I still don't know if she wants children. I could take the choice away from her, rip that fucking IUD out and fuck her until she's pregnant with the next De Luca heir.

As everybody talks amongst themselves, I do a quick google search on my phone. It's advised that a doctor remove an IUD but women have done it themselves. So it's possible. My brother stands over my shoulder looking at my screen as he chuckles, "Tonight, brother. We have so many plans for tonight."

Natalia looks over at us. "What are you two up to?"

Drake chuckles lightly, "Oh nothing for you to worry about, pretty girl."

She arches an eyebrow as she glances between the two of us. "I doubt that with you two psychos."

Oh, you have no idea sweet little sunshine. The plans we have for you tonight will be life altering. Everything will ensure she's ours forever.

DRAKE

Twenty Hours Later…

Natalia stirs and the excitement builds in me like a kid counting down the days to his birthday. Will she be pissed when she realizes what we've done? I'm sure of it. And I can't wait for it. She was such a good girl when Dante handed her a drink and she drank down all the drugs in it. We needed her to be asleep because we knew the pain would be too much for her to bear. Even my little pain slut has her limits. The biggest reason we drugged her is so she wouldn't fight us. There was no chance of us not doing this. I suppose we always knew we would, but it was finally time.

She moans lightly as she wakes up. Natalia looks gorgeous, naked on her stomach, "Oh my god, why does my back hurt so bad?"

Dante hands her a glass of water and two advil, "Take this, sunshine."

Natalia takes the medication and hands the glass back to him as she asks, "What did you two do to me last night, and why can't I remember anything?"

Dante and I help her into a sitting position as she whimpers from the pain. She touches her back with a wince. "What did you do?"

I grin at her. "We marked you, pretty girl. Now everyone will know you belong to us."

She jumps off the bed and runs to the bathroom. We can't see her from here but know she's spotted the brand new tattoo on her lower back when we hear a scream, "What the fuck did you do? Goddamn psychos!"

Dante and I both sit on the bed, waiting for our pretty girl to attack us. It's coming. He knows it and so do I. It's going to be fucking beautiful. I can't wait. However, my brother is a fucking idiot and neither of us sees what's coming.

She charges out at us with a knife that Dante must have left in the bathroom. Natalia holds it up in a threatening stance as her wide, fierce eyes dart between us as if she's deciding who to stab first.

"Put the knife down, baby," Dante says calmly as he holds his hands in the air.

"Who did the tattoo?"

I sigh audibly, "I did."

She steps closer to me. "Give me one reason to not kill you."

Natalia looks so fucking beautiful like this. The anger flowing through her bloodstream is palpable, like a fourth person in the room. This is what I wanted, her standing up for herself, although I don't particularly wish to be stabbed to death.

"Reason number one, you love me."

She narrows her gaze at me and snorts, "Too bad that means nothing. Give me a better reason."

"I love you."

Her expression of anger is quickly replaced with one of shock. "So you drugged me and tattooed me against my will as a sign of love? Or do you do this to all your women? Brand them with your fucking name?"

I attempt to give her a reassuring smile. "No, pretty girl, only you."

Natalia steps even closer to me and presses the tip of the sharp blade into my chest, "Is that supposed to be a comfort to me, asshole?"

"Yes," I answer as my heart races but not from fear but from excitement. Maybe she's right and I am a psycho because I've never been more turned on in my entire life.

"Cut me, pretty girl. If it makes you feel better, slice my skin. I don't mind. In fact, I hope you do because I will rather enjoy punishing you like I never have before."

Her hand shakes slightly. "You're going to kill me?"

I chuckle as I shake my head. "I said punish you, pretty girl. There is nothing you could do that would ever make me end your beautiful life. If you think for one second I'd choose to live without you, think again, pretty girl. My life has been a different experience without you and now with you. I won't go back to knowing what it's like to breathe without you. I'd rather fucking die."

Dante chuckles when the knife slips from her hand and clanks onto the hardwood floor. "I knew that would do it," he mutters under his breath.

Natalia climbs onto my lap. "And you said you couldn't be poetic. I'm still pissed at you, though. You should watch your back in case I change my mind."

I rub my thumb across her bottom lip as she watched me with fascination. "Is that so, pretty girl? Do you think you could live without me? What about my brother? Are you going to kill us both and go on with your life as if we meant nothing to you?"

She kisses the tip of my thumb sweetly. "No. I couldn't bear it even if you are both psychopaths."

Dante chuckles loudly. "I suppose we should get the rest of the truth out of the way."

Natalia glares over my shoulder at my brother as I wrap my arms around her waist, making sure I'm not touching where we've marked her. "What now?"

He admits to her, "I removed your IUD last night."

Her response makes me laugh because I expected her to be upset about him removing it without her consent. "How the hell do you even know how to do that?"

I glance behind me and see him shrug his shoulders, "You Tube, baby. There's literally a video for everything."

She hits me in my chest when I laugh. "Why?"

I kiss her neck softly. "Isn't that obvious, pretty girl? It was impeding you giving us beautiful babies."

"Yeah, that's the point," she groans before adding, "You two really need therapy. Possibly more than the De Luca money can afford because nothing you've done says you're sane men."

She motions for Dante to move closer and he sits beside me and she swings her right leg over his lap. "You are both certifiable. The most insane men I've ever met, but you're mine."

My brother and I both agree, as our words are identical. "And you're ours."

Natalia giggles and asks, "Should we seal this with a kiss?'"

I shake my head. "We'll seal it by fucking you into oblivion."

A sweet little moan escapes from full lips. "Oblivion sounds good. Fuck me into oblivion."

Epilogue

DRAKE

For months we sifted through all the people who had filed kidnapping reports in 1989. There were over one hundred non custodial abductions in the Orlando area during that time that we found. However, only twelve involved infants. *Only.* And three children disappeared from Walt Disney World fitting Natalia's description. It's been an arduous process for her parents to wait for DNA results. However, we were insistent that no one would come near our girl without confirmation that they were indeed her parents.

She does not know that today, Maria and Jacob Maxwell, her parents, are coming to see her. Natalia doesn't even know that we've found them. We both knew the anxiety would eat her alive. We know our girl well and she would've spent days or maybe even weeks wondering if they'd like her. There's no doubt they will. Dante found out from a conversation with them a few weeks ago that it took them three years to conceive her. They were over the moon and doting parents. Until fate dealt them a nasty hand. At only thirty years old, Maria had a seizure while sitting on a bench while her daughter, *Grace,* slept in a stroller and Bebe took her and never looked back. The Maxwells never stopped looking for her; however, there was never a single lead. Of course, once the Grants moved to New York, it made the odds of finding her even worse than they already were. Still, every single year on her birthday, they would go on the news and plead with the public for help to find their daughter. The police told them on her fifth birthday that they were no longer considering it an abduction but a murder. She repeated the words they said to her, "At this point we're considering this a recovery mission," meaning they were looking for a dead body. In eighty-nine percent of abduction cases, children normally died within twenty-four hours of being taken. Still, they never gave up hope. Even after they had two more children, their search for her never wavered.

We sit in the living room waiting for them to arrive. Dante hands her a glass of wine. Natalia smirks at him, "You aren't drugging me again, are you?"

He chuckles, "No sunshine. Not today."

Our security team enters with the Maxwells in tow and instantly Natalia's hands shake, so Dante takes the glass from her hand and sets it on the coffee table. Our girl stares at her mother in shock. *She knows.* We don't need to tell her this is her mother because it's like looking into a damn mirror. They have the same long dark hair, slender waist, wider hips. The only difference is a few fine lines around her eyes. She's an older version of Natalia, but the resemblance is striking.

"Are you?" Natalia asks, knowing the truth but needing confirmation.

She nods, "I'm your mother, Maria. This is your father, Jacob Maxwell. We've been looking for you for nearly your entire life."

The tears are instant for both women. Natalia cries, "I'm sorry. I didn't know. I should have, but I didn't."

Maria goes to step forward and watches Dante and me with caution, "May I?"

"Natalia?" I ask and she nods, "Yes."

She walks over to our girl, who is sitting on the couch, and kneels in front of her. "Do not apologize. Ever. You were an innocent child. None of this is your fault, and how could you have possibly known? They made sure you didn't."

Natalia wrapped her arms around her mother as her father stayed back, watching them, wiping tears from his eyes. And I somehow knew everything was going to be fine. They may have missed twenty-six years together, but nothing will keep them apart again.

Once her parents left and went back to their hotel, we knew we needed to make sure she was okay with everything that had happened.

"Do you think they were uncomfortable with me? Maybe that's why they stayed at a hotel instead of staying here?"

Dante pulls her onto his lap, "No sunshine, I don't think that's it. They want to make sure they don't overcrowd you. Remember, Maria said you'd take this at your pace."

She sinks into his chest as I ask, "Do you think you want to go by Grace or Natalia?"

Turning her head to me, she stares at me with a shocked expression, as if she hadn't even considered that she could choose what people call her. "Do you think it'll upset them if I want to continue being called Natalia? It's all I've ever known."

"Pretty girl, they are so happy to have found you. I think they'll deal with the name and I think they'll understand."

She gasps, "I can't believe you guys did this for me."

I chuckle as I move onto the couch beside them. She runs her fingers across my jaw. "We'd do anything for you, baby."

A giggle escapes past her lips. "Except let me go."

I grin, "Except let you go. That will never happen."

Epilogue Two

NATALIA

One Year Later…

I knew Grace wasn't me, not anymore. I don't recall being called by that name, so it felt foreign. Luckily, my parents understood and agreed to call me Natalia even though it's probably bitter on their tongues considering my kidnappers named me. I did, however, change my name.

Six weeks ago, I became Mrs. De Luca. Unfortunately, I couldn't marry both men because that's illegal. So my marriage certificate says I'm married to Dante, but we had a ceremony where I married both of them. My parents were there once. My mother and I had a heart to heart. She found it unusual that I was romantically linked to two brothers. I can't say I blame her. That she knows they're mafia men didn't help matters. However, the more time she spent with the three of us, the more clear it became that both of my men love me and will do anything for me. What more could you possibly want for your daughter? I want for nothing, my every need is met and the fact that my best friend is now my sister-in-law? Yeah, that doesn't suck.

I stand in the kitchen making lunch for my growing hungry belly when I hear one of my husbands, Drake, yelling over the phone, "No. We are not helping that asshole find his sister. Where was he when we needed to find Dalia?"

I glance over to Dante as he walks over to me and whispers in my ear, "Don't worry, baby, it's just business. Nothing touches the De Lucas."

I hate how confident he sounds because it's as if he doesn't understand the danger that exists by simply being who they are.

"Fuck Aries Lombardo," Drake screams as he disconnects the call and walks over to me. "How's our baby?"

I rub my belly. "Just fine. Is everything okay?"

He grins wide, "Nothing touches the De Lucas, pretty girl. Everybody is safe."

Sure, everybody is always safe, until they aren't. I have a sinking feeling in my stomach and this time it isn't from morning sickness. Everything I want is standing in this kitchen, and if I lose any part of it, I won't survive.

CHELLE ROSE

THE MEN OF MAYHEM SERIES
BOOK FOUR

DE LUCA

THE DALIA EFFECT

Chapter One

DALIA

My brothers live and breathe danger, but I stay away from it. Of course, I know what they do as I knew what my father did. There are women in the mafia but I knew from an early age I would never be one of them. The men in my family would never allow it. I prefer to spend my time helping victims of sexual abuse. Going through what I went through as a child is a gift. Yes, a gift. Not because I enjoyed being raped or watching my mother be raped and eventually die. It's a gift because it makes me understand what they have been through and that you can get through to the other side of it. That's not to say that I'm completely healed. I'm twenty-four and I've never been on a date. I don't trust men other than my brothers. Aries Lombardi has become a thorn in my side as of late. He won't leave me alone and keeps calling me wifey. It's annoying. If ever I were to trust a man, it wouldn't be him and it wouldn't be a man belonging to a rival family.

I wake to a heavy feeling in my head, as if I had way too much to drink last night, but I only had two glasses of wine. Moving my arm, it lands on a hard chest, causing me to scream as I open my eyes and spot a naked Aries lying in bed beside me.

"What the fuck!" I yell as I jump up on the bed, also naked.

However, my nakedness isn't my biggest concern at the moment. It's the giant rock on my left ring finger.

He grins at my shocked face, "Good morning, Wifey. Did you sleep well?"

"Why are you here?" What am I doing here? What's happening?" I ask in a rushed panic.

"Sit," he orders, and I do as I grab the sheet and wrap it around my body.

"Last night, I told you we would be married or your brothers would go to prison. You agreed, so now we're husband and wife."

"Why?" I can't for the life of me understand why he'd want to be married to me or why, if I agreed, I can't remember a damn thing.

He chuckles, "My sister is missing and your idiot brothers have refused to help, but we're family now, so I'm sure they'll have a change of heart."

"You're disgusting."

Aries grabs my arms and tosses me onto my back. Holding my arms above my head, he rubs his cock against my clit, "Tell me how disgusting I am while I make you come."

"Don't!" I yell.

He chuckles, his breath hot against my neck. "Do you not like to come, Dalia?"

"I never have," I squeak like a pathetic little animal.

Aries groans like this is the best news he's ever heard. "Oh baby, you got me a wedding present. Now be a good little wifey and bleed for me."

Acknowledgements:

Thank you to my amazing Alpha, BETA, and ARC Teams.

There are so many people who have offered me unwavering support. Thank you. You know who you are.

To those that said I couldn't, thank you. Because of you, I did.

To the Readers: You will never know what it means to me that you chose to read my book. Thank you from the very bottom of my heart.

ALSO BY CHELLE ROSE:

Forbidden Desires Series

1. *Mercy www.books2read.com/chellerosemercy*
2. *Finding Mercy www.books2read.com/chellerosefinding-mercy*
3. *Liam and Mercy www.books2read.com/LiamandMercy*
4. *Xander's Secret https://books2read.com/Xanderssecret*

Dark Desires Series

1. *Unholy www.books2read.com/chelleroseunholy*
2. *Unhinged www.books2read.com/chelleroseunhinged*
3. *Unchained www.books2read.com/chelleroseunchained*
4. *Undone www.books2read.com/chelleroseundone*
5. *An Unhinged Wedding www.books2read.com/unhingedwedding*

Men of Mayhem Series

1. *De Luca: The Devil www.books2read.com/delucathedevil*
2. *De Luca: The Saint www.books2read.com/delucasaint*
3. *De Luca: The Sinister Game www.books2read.com/sinistergame*

Printed in Great Britain
by Amazon

49821740R00126